THE SIX KINGDOMS
THE HIGH KING OF CARRAIG

JOHN T. MCDONALD

authorHOUSE®

AuthorHouse™
1663 Liberty Drive
Bloomington, IN 47403
www.authorhouse.com
Phone: 1 (800) 839-8640

Published by AuthorHouse 08/30/2019

ISBN: 978-1-7283-2509-5 (sc)
ISBN: 978-1-7283-2508-8 (e)

Library of Congress Control Number: 2019912748

Print information available on the last page.

TABLE OF CONTENTS

CHAPTER I

THE ISLAND OF CARRAIG

The island of Carraig is the center point of the six known kingdoms. Each kingdom is its own land mass surrounded by one of the three seas. Carraig is split into four sections, the North, the South, the East, and the West. In the North there are many woods with trees that climb to the sky. There are crystal clear streams full of fish and fresh water so pure; all that is needed to drink from them is a cup. The coastline of the North is a little more treacherous. This place is known as the Cliffs of Seirbigh. A deadly drop off, over four hundred feet, right into the Sea of Oir Agus Airgid.

On the opposite side of Carraig in the South there is also a coastline that has claimed many lives; known as the Cliffs of Dungan. These cliffs do not have a far drop, only about one hundred feet. However, at the bottom, lay razor sharp rocks that are heavily beaten by the Sea of Dtonnta Arda. Many years ago the High King would force traitors and thieves to jump to their deaths from these cliffs. Two miles north of this wall of rock is the Southern Capital, Castle de Sinna. Within a five mile radius of the Capital are the homes of many southern Carraigians. Mostly farmers and fisherman reside here. There is a harbor to the southeast where a few sailors conduct trade with passing ships. It is common for kingdoms to trade with one another in peace time. Some kingdoms have been known to still trade or sell with one another even during war times; as long as the war doesn't involve the two parties directly. Carraig being one of the largest and more dominant kingdoms, seldom has fought with other kingdoms, although it has happened in the past. Carraig has been known for its civil wars amongst its own countrymen in the past.

On the eastside of the island is the Castle of Sechnaill. This is the wealthiest of castles due to its trade with the Kingdom to the far east. Across the Sea of Arrachtaigh, the Kingdom of Aodhan sails to the East Harbor of Carraig. This occurs a few times in a month. There is one hundred miles of water between the Kingdom of Aodhan and the Kingdom of Carraig. This is the closest distance between any of the five island Kingdoms. The Castle of Sechnaill has many villagers; blacksmiths are more common in this area, although mining has become popular with some in this region. Many mountains surround the eastern side of Carraig and these minors have discovered gems that do well with the trade of Aodhan in the harbor.

Castle of Findliath is the Capital of the West on the Island of Carraig. Hunters thrive in this dense forest, and the women sew amazing garments. Ten foot tall grizzly bears have been seen on multiple occasions in these woods. Countless hunters have failed to return home from this thick and wild wood. The west side of Carraig also has a harbor but is rarely used. Only a few months in the summer does anyone dare to venture out into these deep waters. Whales the size of castles and sharks that have been mistaken as ships, dwell near this part of the island.

There are only a few roads on Carraig, connecting the four castles and a few side roads that lead to the four harbors. The villages are never too far from a capital, therefore roads are not needed. There is one other means of travel from north to south. On the northeast side there is the beginning of a river never wider than a few hundred yards. It flows southeast through the island past the East Capital and down to the South Capital. There are a few bargemen that charge a few silver coins to ferry people down and back up the river. Some fishermen have their own boats and travel this river frequently.

The laws in Carraig are very simple; only kill in self defense, no stealing, cheating, or rape. Serve your King, Capital, and defend Carraig with your life. The property you own is yours to do with as you please, this includes slaves. Slaves in Carraig are usually used for farming and have a separate house on the property of their owner. In times of war, slaves are put at the front lines with long sharp spears to stop any riders on horseback that might be leading a charge. The East Capital has the largest amount of slaves, purchased mostly from traders that have sailed from the Kingdom of Aodhan. Slaves are comprised of mostly men who have committed a crime not entirely worthy of death. Over the years slaves have been less commonly used as a means of trade, due to a less amount of controversial wars between capitals.

Until very recently Carraig was ruled by the High King Aengus, of the North Capital, and he resided in the Castle de Sumerled. Aengus ruled as High King for sixty years, he took the role as High King when he killed the King of the South Capital in hand to hand combat. At that time Aengus was King of the North and had been for two years due to his father being slain in battle. The King of the South declared himself High King and Aengus believing it to be his birth right challenged him. After successfully defeating the King of the South, Aengus took up the place of High King. The East and West Kings did not deny him this position. Aengus did not want to compete for rule over Carraig, so after the East and West Kings died of old age twenty or so years later, Aengus appointed lords to take over in the other Capitals. This made him the only King of Carraig.

Aengus was good to the people of Carraig; he made sure market places where guarded. Thieves were dealt with in severe ways. If someone stole their hand would be removed from their body. If they tried to run their feet would be removed. If someone tried to cheat or lie about what they were selling their tongue would be cut out. These barbaric methods of upholding the law worked very well. Crime was almost obsolete. There were a few bandits that lived and traveled in the woods but if their crimes got to out of hand; a hunting party would be organized and the outlaws would be taken to the Cliffs of Dungan and cast over.

Aengus fought in a few battles earning himself the title "The Bear King". It is said that Aengus would leap from his horse down on his enemy with a large branch grasped with both hands, on one side of the branch there was an axe and on the other a large square hammer. The heads of his enemy's would explode upon impact; leaving only their body's for display. He also wore a bear skin over his armor with a crown that would fit over the head of the bear. He had this custom made in the Eastern Capital. His enemies would only see what appeared to be a giant bear flying through the air biting the heads off of soldiers in his path. Aengus was victorious in all of his battles gaining the respect of his people and his army's.

Aengus would travel every few months to a different Capital, visiting and being updated on events that had occurred by the lord of the Capital. He did this during non winter months. During the winter he would stay in the North Capital because it would often get to cold to camp in transition to a different Capital. Aengus married a girl from the North Capital when she was eighteen and he closer to thirty. She was the daughter of a land owner who had a very successful life. This land owner also fought with Aengus during all of his battles. Aengus had four children with his wife Queen Ethel. Four boys, huge boys, not one was under six foot three inches and two hundred and fifty pounds. The oldest was John and two years under him came James then Michael and Daniel.

These boys became the highlight of Aengus's life. He personally taught them everything from hunting, fishing, sword play, and how to rule a kingdom by being fair and just. When the boys reached twenty years old he made them each a lord of Carraig. He gave James the West Capital at Castle of Findliath, Michael the East Capital at Castle of Sechnaill, and Daniel the South Capital at Castle de Sinna. The oldest son John stayed with Aengus in the North

Capital; this is to be his as well as High King when Aengus is no more.

Each of the sons married and had children of their own. John married Elaine and had two boys Brian and Cahal. James married Rahkel and had two girls Aileen and Colleen. Michael married Mimi who died giving birth to their daughter Cara. Daniel married Abigail who bore their two sons Art and Braden. The brother's would travel to one another's Capital at random and unannounced. This was most likely to see which of the three were more hospitable. This lasted a few years until word of an army traveling by sea, stopping at different Kingdoms pillaging and burning villages reached Carraig's ears. This army was said to take the men and women as slaves. High King Aengus called the lords to the North Capital and ordered them to gather their army's and start patrols along the shores of Carraig. These patrols were immediately put into action. Everything from marching army's to one or two foot soldiers were put on watch.

The entire Kingdom of Carraig was notified and put on alert. These warnings had come from a trading ship that pulled into the East Harbor coming from the Kingdom of Aodhan. The merchants from that vessel said they had heard stories of this from others they trade with. Although there was no sign of such a ship, the High King still demanded the patrols stay in effect. Over a year the patrols began to thin out and the army's began to pack up camp and start making their way back to their homes.

It was the end of winter at that time and the first day of spring was upon Carraig. Early one morning three riders were sent out of the North Capital in route to the other three

Capitals. The High King Aengus of the North Capital was dead. He died at age eighty two. John, now the King of the North sent the messengers out to inform his brothers. Along with the news of his father's death he informed his messengers to spread the word to the nearby villages of the Capitals that he was now the High King of Carraig.

CHAPTER II

THE CHANGE OF TRADITION

I t had been ten days since the messengers were sent out from the North Capital. The ceremonial feast of the High King's demise is set to be held in five days. It takes three days to reach the East and West Capitals and six days to reach the South Capital at a moderate pace on horseback with a light load. It is custom for the messengers to ride back with the party unto who the message had been delivered. Yet no sign of either East or West Capitals had been spotted on the roads. John began to wonder if his messengers had arrived at their destinations. "Where are my brothers?" John asked to his Captain of the archers Curtis. John being twenty eight years old now and having no true experience as a King made him question himself. Curtis on the other hand was thirty eight, John looked to Curtis not only as one of his fiercest Captains and warriors but as an advisor as well. Curtis was very tall and wide, his arm's the size of tree trunks and his chest bulged with power. He had long dark hair and a long dark beard that climbed down his chest. His eyes were dark and had seen the cruel heartbreak of battle. Curtis had fought in a battle with Aengus, and he was said to be such a great warrior that Aengus made him a Captain only a day after the battle had begun. That particular battle lasted three months and Curtis fighting side by side with Aengus is the reason the victory came so quickly most believe.

"The East and West Capitals should have been here by now my King" Curtis replied with concern. "And the South should be arriving in a few days. If no one has arrived in the next three days I will put together a group of soldiers and travel to the Capitals myself" Curtis said with a hint of agitation in his voice. "No, I will go if no one arrives. You will stay here and rule in my place until I return. Perhaps my brothers are bringing with them a large collection of people for this occasion; my father was well liked by his people. Most would consider it a privilege to honor his death" John stated with pride.

John is kind at heart yet he has a sense of dominance when he walks into a room. Not only because he was a Prince of Carraig and now the High King, he held this trait even when he was just a young lad. His shoulders are broad and his arms are strong, King John doesn't need to raise his voice to get his point across. However, in the rare case that he does, his voice echoes like thunder and his gaze pierces like lightning in a pitch black sky. John's eyes are blue with designs in them that look like electricity. His scowl strikes fear in the hearts of men, yet his smile can bring out the best in any man or woman. John is slow to anger and quick to forgive. The ideal trait's for a High King of Carraig.

"Elaine, are the rooms in order? Enough for the entire family?" asked John. "Of course my love, they have been for nearly three days now" Elaine said back to John. Elaine, now the Queen of Carraig took on the task of preparing the Castle of Sumerled for the extended stay of numerous guests. She enjoyed this job, not only was this opportunity going to be recognized by all of the guests that would be staying, but John would notice this heartfelt gesture as well. Elaine loved pleasing John in every way that she could; from the simplest acts of showing her affection, to the extravagant ceremonies such as this. Her beauty is like no others in all six Kingdoms. Her long blonde hair glistens in the sun and her blue eyes sparkle like pools of water. Most men bow their heads when in her presence, not because she is the Queen now, but simply because her gorgeous smile would put them in a daze.

John was now sitting in his father's chair in front of a large fire place. The mouth of this fire place stretched over twenty feet long and four feet high. There are two chairs placed in front of it. One was Aengus's the other was John's. The two would sit here for many hours while Aengus would tell stories of his life and the life of his father to John. Behind these two chairs sat a long table made of oak that can accommodate around thirty men. This table is in the center of the room. This room has been known to contain more than two hundred people. It is known as the great hall. On the sides of the room there are other smaller tables that line up all around this magnificent stone room. The ceiling is so high that some have mistaken it for the night sky. There are many rooms in this castle but none as large as this. This room is where all of Aengus's son's were married. On the upper levels of the castle are huge guest rooms enough for five hundred if the occasion called for it. On the lower levels are where the soldiers quarters are located. Four soldiers to a room, and about one hundred rooms. There is also an extravagant kitchen adjacent from the great hall. This is where many feasts have been prepared and then served to be devoured in the great hall.

Elaine sat in the chair next to John. "What is on your mind? You look troubled, your father is very proud of you. Celebrate to his long life and his strong rein, do not grieve over his death" she said with her head tilted down and her eyes heavy. John replied with "I wasn't as ready to rule as I had thought to be". He gave a small grin and said "I suppose I don't have much of a choice, the old man never did anything expected; such as give me a warning the night before that I would be the new High King when I woke up". They both laughed for a second, but it was soon silenced when a loud bell began to ring.

John quickly jumped to his feet and began to move towards the stairwell that led to the wall; which circled the front of the castle. The back of the castle only had one or two guards at a time, mostly to serve as look outs for ships. They too had a bell. The bells would be rung to alert the Capital of a large group of men closing in on the castle. Since there was no possible way for anyone to climb the Cliffs of Seirbigh; the back of the castle had never rung its bell. It would take more than ten ships closing in on the cliffs for that loud gong to be heard.

Elaine followed closely behind John as he climbed the large stone steps. Once he reached the top there was Curtis bellowing out to the soldiers "Get the archers in their positions! Get the spear men lining the wall! Begin to boil the oil!" "Can you see the colors of the flags?" John said to Curtis very calmly. "Not yet. They are still too far out" Curtis replied. It was standard procedure for the soldiers to arm up and prepare for battle when any large number approached the Capital.

John looked down at the stairs to see a little man with a loud voice looking back at him. "Sire, the foot soldiers are assembled and ready to march" the man hollered as he reached the top of the wall. This was the second of the three Captains. "Good work Aaron. Any word on Simon and his riders?" John asked, again in a calm voice. "They are still mounting up in the stables, they should be ready momentarily my King" Aaron stated. Aaron was only five foot nine inches and carried an axe almost as big as he was. He was strong enough to wield it and fierce enough no one in the entire North Capital would challenge him. He was said to be a funny man after he had a few ales in him. He is the Captain of the foot soldiers and his men are loyal to him. His men are fierce and brutal when need be and would gladly give their lives for King and Country.

Just then another loud voice broke through the commotion; it was coming from the open area down in the lower level where the market place was usually set up. It was just an empty plot of dirt with soldiers scrambling to get to their assigned areas once the first bell had been rung. "The riders are ready my King!" it was Simon the third Captain. This man was known for his skill of fighting on the back of a horse. Whether it be a spear, sword, bow and arrow or axe it did not matter with Simon he was excellent with all of them. He had the favor of all the young ladies that resided in the Capital. His long light brown hair and smooth face with a white smile and strong eyes was enough to have all the maidens start to giggle when he walked past. However, it was his talent for killing his enemies that earned him his right to lead.

John yelled down loud enough for Simon to hear him "Have them stand by and wait for my order!" Simon replied quickly with "As you command!" John looked on down the road that led south. The number of people, horses, and wagons grew and grew. It was far enough away that it looked like a trail of black ants coming up the road, a never ending trail. John began to get nervous; perhaps this wasn't one of his brothers. The trail of men should be less than half that size. Still John kept looking in silence, just when he was prepared to send out a scout rider, Elaine interrupted his thoughts. "It appears that the whole Kingdom of Carraig is coming. Should I have the kitchens light the fires my love?" she asked. "Not yet darling, I want to hear the trumpets play first" John said looking at her with a smile. Hearing one of the East, West, or South Capitals trumpets play announcing their presence would put his mind at ease.

Another ten minutes went by when someone on the wall yelled "Riders approaching!" three riders had left the main party and were sprinting up the road. None of the riders had a flag with them; therefore no one could make out where they were from. The riders were now in plain sight and still riding hard. About one mile from the castle gates they stopped, formed a line and rose what appeared to be trumpets. The first rider began to play; it was the Lord of the South Capital's tune. Followed by that, was the second rider, this tune belonged to the Lord of the West Capital.

Then the last rider played the sound of the East. It was all three of John's brothers riding in together as one giant party. John looked at his Captains and shouted with a huge smile "Send out a welcome party!" he then looked at Elaine with a grin and said to her "Start the fires in the kitchen, and have the wine and ale sellers opened" she ran with excitement almost forgetting to breathe. John had a smile of relief and joy on his face. The entire North Capital was ready for the celebration feast of the new High King and the memory of the old.

CHAPTER III

THE REUNITING OF
THE BROTHERS

T he gates lowered and the flags of the Capitals flew high. The first to enter was the Lord of the West, James. Followed in a wagon behind him were his wife and two girls and behind them were men and women from the West Capital. It was a mixture of land owners, farmers, villagers, and soldiers. Next was Lord Michael of the East riding next to his daughter Cara and behind them were the men and women of the East. Lord Daniel rode in with his two sons Art and Braden; behind him was his wife Abigail in a wagon with her servants. The men and women of the South followed closely behind.

Four thousand people showed up all at once. The family of the lord's and their personal guard and servants were given rooms in the castle. The rest of the people of Carraig began setting up tents outside of the castle gates. The market place was reformed and people flocked in and out of the castle grounds. Some had relatives in nearby villages and would eventually ride back with them to stay in their homes instead of tents. In a matter of three hours the North Capital had more life in it than anyone had seen in years.

John was sitting at the head of the oak table. Directly to his right was Elaine and to his left sat his oldest son Brian. Next to Brian was Cahal, John's youngest son, then sat Daniel, Michael, and James along with their families. After that were John's three Captains and their families. The entire great hall was filled with music, dancing, food, and drink. At the same time, outside in the tents were experiencing much of the same. Everyone was laughing and telling stories. There hadn't been that much ale and wine drunk in a single night in the history of Carraig. Nor had there been that many children conceived either.

Later into the night John and the lords went outside to the center of the castle. On a huge mound of sticks and wood surrounded by dry hay, lay the body of their father Aengus. With a few words spoken from each of the brothers, John set the mound ablaze. The laughter and noise from the tents silenced and nothing could be heard but a few babies' crying and a dog barking in the distance. The fire lasted about two hours until nothing but the orange glow of a few embers remained.

John stated "Well, he's in our memories and our hearts now. Let's all go back inside and enjoy the rest of the night" his brothers agreed and they all walked together, back into the great hall. Soon after, the laughter rose again and the low rumble of a big crowd outside could be heard. After many hours in the great hall the people slowly started to retire to their chambers. Only a few low voices could be heard near a few dim fires outside of a couple different tents. Finally the Capital slept.

The next morning was slow to come for most. However, by early afternoon the market place was full again. Selling, buying, and trading were happening all throughout the Capital. The people from the west would trade and sell furs and salted meat, the people from the east would trade and sell weapons and jewels, and the north and south would trade a mixture of everything. For the most part everyone was getting along, which wasn't always the case. But for the time being everything was good for the Kingdom of Carraig.

Three days and nights of this continued and on the forth morning the four brothers convened next to the fire place in the great hall. James was the first to speak "John, I know you have been waiting to lead Carraig for a long time. We were made lords and you were still under fathers rule. However, we have all talked with each other and we all feel that now that father is gone we should go back to the times of old and each be the King of our Capitals". Michael and Daniel looked hopefully at John but didn't dare to speak out of turn. John's cheerful smile slowly turned into a stern face and he said "Why do you feel this way? You all think I cannot lead or you want more power?" "It's not that we feel you can't lead, it's just... father wanted only one King. He did a great job as only one King but even father didn't know what was going on in the other Capitals until he would visit every couple of months" Michael said with the utmost respect in his voice. Daniel slowly began to speak while John had his hand on his chin pondering the proposition "It would be easier on you only having to worry about the

North" Daniel continued with "and nothing would really change" James quickly followed by saying "Father wanted to be the only King because the other Capitals were ruled by other families. That's not the case now; our family will always rule Carraig".

"Tell me then brothers, what happens if the ships that father spoke of reach our shores? What will all of you do then? Will you all band your army's together? Who will command this one massive army?" John questioned them with hostility in his voice. The other brothers looked at him in shame. James spoke up after a small time of silence "If something of that nature occurred, then we would meet together and vote on a decision. Our intention is not to over throw you my brother. Our intention is to make things easier on us as Kings". Michael chimed in right after "It is your decision brother, you are the High King and the only way to change that would be to challenge you or go to war with you and none of us would ever do that". "Think about it brother, it has been great seeing you these last few days. We will now have our men and women gather their things and begin the long journey home" Daniel said in an attempt to change the subject.

The brothers stood up and began to head out of the great hall. Before they reached the massive doorway John called out "I will be visiting each of the Capitals in a few months. If you desire to be Kings, then so be it. When each of you crosses the boarders into your Capitals you are king. Spread the word". With a holler of excitement the brothers made for their horses. Everyone now packed up and ready for the long march back to their homes grabbed the last of their items and said their farewells. John and Elaine were at the wall watching while the line was being formed. The trumpet of the West blew and James and his personal guard led the legion of people down the road.

Elaine looked at John and sighed in relief "it was fun but I'm glad it's over" "Me too, maybe this headache from all the ale will go with them" John laughed. Brian came up the stairs to watch them leave. "Art said he was going to be a King someday. Is that true father?" he asked. "Yes, one day he will be King of the South, and you, King of the North" John replied back to Brian. "I thought there was only one king" Brian stated curiously. "I have changed things back to the old ways my son, at least for the time being" John said with a smile as he looked down at Brian. Elaine smiled at both of them and said "Brian, don't you have chores to be doing? As soon as they leave sight, off with you" "Yes mother" Brian said in an unwilling voice. As the last wagon and rider were out of sight, the Capital began to clean the unruly mess that had been created by this memorable event. Everyone including John did their part in trying to get the place back in order the way it was before the mass amount of friends and family arrived.

Three weeks had passed now and the cleanup had finally come to an end. Things were getting back to normal. With all of the people who had come, the food and coin had multiplied and everyone was still on a joyful note. The nearby villages started bringing in fish and elk to trade. John was content with the decision he had made. It would be easier on him as King of the North rather than High King. Elaine stood by him in this decision as well as the rest of the Kingdom. For a High King to give away some of his power was not easy. By John doing this he earned a little more respect within the people. Of course this wasn't his intention; he only wanted to make his brothers happy. He spent a lot of time in the great hall sitting in his father's chair. Sometimes Brian would sit with him and he would tell a story or two of Aengus, but it was too soon and the memory of his father would sadden him and he would talk of something else.

John would stay up some nights while the castle slept. He would visit the soldiers on their post, only on the castle walls, if he left the castle walls he would have to wake his personal guard to go with him. Not because there was a threat but it was a custom that he dare not change. His father would do this frequently. John was usually accompanied by his two dogs, Roman who was black and Cain who was white. Both had been trained for battle, although they had never seen it. They are a breed from a different Kingdom; they are very tall for dogs and their hair very scraggly and thick. A villager traded for them a few years back and gave them to Aengus as a gift. Aengus not wanting to take on two new pups gave them to John. John gladly took them, and had them trained on their first birthday. The training took several seasons, but he was exceptionally happy when he got them back. They would only listen to his commands and followed him everywhere. Elaine wasn't pleased with this but she too got used to them.

John walked up to a guard on the wall and asked "How's it going up here?" the guard replied in a shaky voice "Good sire" "How old are you boy?" John questioned. The boy replied "Just turned seventeen. I passed my soldier quest yesterday sire" a soldier quest was the last step in becoming a soldier. The other soldiers would take the new prospect into the woods and leave him for three days. On the third day they would attack usually four on the one. Only with dull blades but it was still enough to determine if a soldier was ready for combat or would crumble under pressure. "Congratulations to you" John said while remembering his quest. "Thank you King John" the boy said while raising his chin. They talked about their quest they had and the oaths they had taken directly after, swearing to protect the King, the people, and Carraig.

John introduced the boy to his dogs and the boy introduced himself back. The boy said to Roman and Cain "I am Harold" and he gave a bow. When he rose back up, he noticed a light in the distance coming up the road. "King John, please excuse me but I must alert my company master" Harold said with a sense of urgency in his voice. Good lad, John thought to himself. Who would be riding up at this late hour? He continued to question himself.

A loud "Holt!" that could be heard a mile away came from a soldier at the top of the gate. The rider so out of breath couldn't answer. "Who are you!" the soldier yelled. "Do you know what hour it is?" the soldier continued. After a minute went by the rider caught his breath and said "I am a messenger from the Kingdom of Aodhan! I need to speak to the High King Aengus". "You may not! King Aengus is dead, you can speak with King John in the morning!" the soldier said in a cocky tone of voice. "This message can't wait until morning, the longer I take the more of my people will die!" the rider said in a voice of horror. John had been standing close by hearing the whole conversation. "Let him in, and escort him to the great hall, bring him food and water" John said in an intimidating whisper. "Open the

Gate" the soldier said to another group of soldiers on the lower level.

John sat the messenger in the chair next to his father's in front of the fire place. John sat next to him and asked in a kind voice "What is this message you have for me?" the messenger had fear in his eyes and was very pale. He began to speak quickly "I have been sent here to beg for your help. Aodhan is under attack. Men in ships have sailed to Aodhan; they took the Castle of Aodhan in three days time. Our King and what was left of the army retreated north through the woods of Stillhet, then the plains of Gronn and then through the woods of Dyr where they are setting up at the old abandoned Castle of Alexander. Messengers have been sent throughout Aodhan to spread word to all and rally at Alexander. I was sent here aboard our last ship that wasn't captured by the men that attacked us. I was sent to Carraig to ask the High King for his help". "Stop" John said firmly. "Who are these men? My father spoke of them nearly two years ago. Yet that was the last we had heard" John asked. "These men are said to come from the Kingdom of Adalrikr. They were out cast from their great army. They stole a few ships and went southwest to the Kingdom Dolg. Once they arrived they killed everyone in sight, they stole more ships and whatever else they could find. They made it as far as Hag before returning to their homeland. They stayed there for a year and then got back in their ships and went north through the sea of Dtonnta Arda all the way to Aodhan. They pulled into port and began killing, burning, and stealing all of our assets. Some were taken as slaves, the rest are dead. Our scouts say their leader is staying in the Castle of Aodhan. They say his army continues to grow. It is only a matter of time before they come north to Alexander and the way they fight and the way they continue to get more ships and warriors into Aodhan it is hopeless without the help of Carraig" the messenger claimed in a shaky voice.

"I carry a stamped seal from my King. We are begging you King John. If you don't help us, Aodhan will be no more. Then they will turn west to Carraig. You must help" the messenger said in despair. John looked at the fire place and thought of what to do. He wondered if he should help a Kingdom who he barley even knew. "Why would I risk the lives of my men for Aodhan?" he thought to himself. "I could wait and prepare, so when they do come we are ready" he continued to ponder. Then he remembered something his father had said "A good King helps his people in a time of need but a great King helps them before there is a need" John began to think of what would happen if these men were to invade Carraig. His soldiers were trained for battle and most of them longed for it. His villagers, farmers, women, and children were not and would be swallowed up in the destruction of his lands if he let it get that far. John looked at the messenger with eyes no one had ever seen worn by John, the eyes of war.

CHAPTER IV

WHO WILL FIGHT

The next morning ten messengers from the North Capital were sent out. Two went to the East Capital, two went to the West, two to the South, and two went to the northwest shore. Two went to the northeast shore to work their way down the coast alerting everyone they came across that Carraig was at war. The messengers told everyone they came across to rally at the North Capital no later than six days by order of King John of the North Capital. John sent the messenger from Aodhan back to the Castle of Alexander, to inform the King there, Carraig would fight.

John dressed in his battle gear, gear that glistened in the light; it had gold lined around the arms and legs as well as his helmet. His helmet had one piece that came down in front of his nose; it wrapped around the back of his head and stopped after covering each one of his ears. The top had black horse hair protruding from it. This was hair from his father's horse. He had never been to a battle much less a war.

He was ready, for he knew his father was looking down on him from the heavens of the kings.

Two days had passed since the messengers had been sent out. Already one thousand men were camped outside the castle walls ready for war. John had spoken to Elaine earlier that day telling her that if anything happened to him, Brian was to be crowned King when he came of age. John looked at her with mixed feelings; he was ready for war and his first battle. He perhaps wasn't ready to part with her. She began to weep but he told her to be strong that he couldn't bear to see her like that. Then he left her in their chambers and proceeded to the great hall were his Captains stood waiting with maps of Aodhan. Curtis stood over a map that was placed on the oak table with the other Captains, Simon and Aaron. John walked in with his dogs following close behind; they too were wearing battle armor "Any news on the other Capitals?" John asked in a rushed voice. Simon quickly replied with "two thousand men were said to have left the South, not two days ago my lord" Aaron jumped in with "A scout said the West set out this morning and the East yesterday" "Good, everyday counts. Are the ships all launched into the water? John asked still sounding rushed. "Yes my lord. We will leave the North Harbor as soon as possible; traveling through the Sea of Arrachtaigh into the port of Alexander. I sent five scouts with the messenger from Aodhan, so we should have a good idea of the enemy's whereabouts and movements" Curtis stated in an attempt to reassure John.

It was getting dark when a horn began to blow. It was the trumpet of the East. "They must have ridden all day and night to get here this quickly my lord" Aaron hollered with excitement. Michael burst into the great hall minutes after the horn blew. "Brother! Tell me what has happened. Why are we going to war in another Kingdom?" Michael said with confusion. "We must go to war to prevent the invasion of Carraig" John replied with sincerity. "How many men did you bring?" asked John. "Two thousand, some farmers and blacksmiths but they will help" replied Michael. The two brothers talked more throughout the night. John told Michael of the messenger and the horror the invading army brought with them. He explained that if Aodhan were to be left to their own fate; Carraig would surely be next. Michael sat with John and thought long and hard of this enormous decision in front of them. Michael had no intention of watching his people suffer from an invasion. Yet he didn't want his soldiers lives lost at sea or on foreign soil either. Michael's thoughts haunted him in his chambers while he waited for the other brothers to arrive. Meanwhile, with his mind made up; John prepared for the journey and the battle. However, he did make time for his wife and children. In his own way he explained the importance of the mission and his goals to them. The children seemed fascinated by the idea, while Elaine seemed concerned. She knew this could ultimately lead to her husband's death. With sad eyes she agreed with everything John said and with every passing night she held him a little tighter.

Two days later the other brothers arrived each with two thousand plus men. They met in the great hall and discussed the plans. James was not on the side of John when it came to this war. He tried very hard to convince John to set up patrols again like his father had done before. Michael didn't want to go either he liked James's idea better. Daniel on the other hand was indecisive. Daniel wanted to be in a battle so bad, yet the idea of leaving his homeland bothered him. "Some have never made it through that Sea before" Daniel said to John. "We will make it just fine" John snapped back already annoyed that they were spending time arguing about even going instead of making battle plans on which of their army's would attack from which angle. "This is not our fight. We need to worry about Carraig, not Aodhan" James said in a persuading voice. This went back and forth between the brothers until late that night. Finally James said "Let's vote on it" and for once that day they all agreed.

"All for war" James said not raising his hand. John's hand went up alone. "Staying here and patrolling our shores" James said quietly while lifting his hand a few inches above his head. Daniel lifted his hand slowly not looking at John. Then all eyes went to Michael. John looked at Michael with hope; this was his little brother that always would follow him around. This was his little brother he had taught how to ride a horse. Michael looked at John with shame in his eyes and slowly lifted his hand. That was it; the vote for war across the Sea to Aodhan was over. "Sorry John, I just think it is safer to stay here" Michael said. "I will see you all when I return. Brian will act as King of the North until I get back" John said while standing up from the oak table. "Curtis! Ready the men of the North. We ride to North Harbor tonight" John bellowed in a disappointed yet commanding voice.

Michael looked sadly at John as he put on his helmet and left the great hall. Michael went to his men and yelled "If there are any men of the East that wish to fight for King John then go now!" James and Daniel did the same and out of six thousand men only five hundred volunteered. Michael went to John as he was climbing on his horse and said "I will send five hundred men to the North to patrol and stand watch. Be careful brother" "I will be back shortly" John said with a confidence in his voice that made Michael look up at him in awe.

Michael had never felt so guilty, if John was still the only King of Carraig there would have been no vote. The High King's word was the law and now because Michael had stood by his other brothers instead of John this could be his doom. Michael watched his brother John ride away with over two thousand men behind him leading a charge for war. This made the hair on the back of Michael's neck stand high. John didn't look back, not once; he had said his goodbyes to Elaine and his boys. Now he was ready for battle, ready for the cold taste of death in the air he had heard so much about. John was nervous yet fearless as he rode to North Harbor to board the ships.

James gathered his men and started to make his way back to the West. He did not wait for Daniel or Michael. He left some of his men behind as well to catch up. James was feeling his father's gaze upon him, a gaze of disappointment and disgust. Daniel was second to leave the North Capital. He too felt sadness over him. As if a part of his soul had fled from his view. At one point he considered turning back and riding to his brother's aide. He glanced back at Abigail's wagon were he knew she slept. He then looked behind again this time towards his two boys who were riding together twenty feet away. If he turned back now and went for John that might be the last glance at his family he ever saw. He continued to ride for the South Capital; it was silent going down the dark road.

Michael had left Cara with his servant girls. He too was in controversy with himself. His only child already motherless would grow up alone without parents if he were to ride for Aodhan. Michael admired John's bravery. Michael was not afraid of battle, he was afraid of being so far from his daughter. Still he felt shame in not following the brother that paid so much attention to him in their youth. It was too late now; all he could do was wait for word on his brother's quest.

John and his men were riding hard to the North Harbor. John was not dwelling on his brother's decision to avoid war. He was focused on his mission. Next to him on his right was Curtis riding hard with a wild and maniacal look on his face. He, unlike some, had been waiting for another chance to swing his sword. Much like him to John's left was Simon also with a face of blood thirsty lust. Directly behind John was Aaron. Aaron was more interested in the comfort of his saddle, he was not the greatest of riders and the continuous up and down motion did not settle well according to the expression on his face.

The other soldier's were behind their leader's four men across. Some were ready for battle, they had dreamed about it since young boys. Others were scared and wanted to turn home but the penalty for traitors is death. The older men looked at the younger with kind eyes some saying "If you stick by me I'll keep you safe while you get the hang of things" others said things not as comforting such as "If you get in my way boy I'll kill you myself" overall, the morale was high. All the men were concerned about the voyage across the Sea. Only a few had every traveled farther than a few miles out. This time of year however the Seas were most calm.

Through the dark John spotted lanterns from what appeared to be North Harbor. He looked at Curtis and said "Almost there, I can see the harbor and the ships are ready!" Curtis looked back at him with a smile and replied "We are with you brother! We will be like a wave crashing upon the Cliffs of Seirbigh!" the two laughed with a devilish tone as they approached the Harbor.

CHAPTER V

ACROSS THE SEA OF ARRACHTAIGH

J ohn and his men reached the North Harbor. John looked at the ships and was not pleased with the ships that had been put in the Sea. These ships had been brought on shore and stored for many years. It was a nearby woodsman's job to keep the ships maintained and ready to be deployed in times like these. That woodsman had died three years past and no one even knew because the last time any of those ships were inspected John was still a boy. The ships were more long wide boats with thirty or so ores and one sail. There were no places to sleep only bench seats going from one side to the other. The front had a ramp that could come down to the ground when the ship was beached. It had a long platform in the front where horses could stand. These platforms were not big enough to fit more than ten horses per ship.

John looked at these ships with dismay. "We are going to have to send most of our horses back to the Capital" he said to Simon. "Only your riders and I can take horses to Aodhan" John said shaking his head yet still looking forward to the Sea. "I will spread the word my King" Simon replied with haste. The ships began to be loaded with soldiers and their weapons along with fresh water jugs and bread. Bread was the only food source that would keep unspoiled besides the bags of dried and salted meat. It wouldn't make the best meal but putting the dried meat on the bread was better than nothing. Goats were too loud and hard to control for a voyage across the sea. Let alone trying to cook on the one fire pit located by the tiller, during the rock of the sea. None the less the men would make due, mostly because they had no choice. John informed Curtis that upon their return, new ships were to be built. John would not see this disaster again in his life time.

After many hours had passed the ships were finally loaded and ready to set sail. John's ship led the way. With him he had his three Captains and his personal guard. They also had horses and an old fisherman that offered to go; saying he knew the way to the Castle of Alexander. He was confident enough that John trusted him. John had seen this fisherman from time to time and knew he had spent most of his time on the sea.

"My brothers Capitals use their ships, why couldn't we be leaving out of there" John said looking at Simon while grinning. "They might have better ships; at least we know where we're going. Most of them get lost and never come back" Simon said in rebuttal. John laughed and said "You're right they don't have an eighty year old blind man who can't hear leading them around the Sea" they both chuckled for a moment and then starred into the black sky. There was a small breeze coming up into their faces and the only sound that could be heard was the slight splash of water coming off the bow's of the ships as they cut through the water.

That first night at sea was peaceful for the men. They relaxed and the slight rock of the waves put most of their uneasy minds to rest. Early the next morning right when the sun started to emit its powerful glow, John woke. He looked around at his men sleeping while sitting up, some leaning on the one next to them and Curtis behind the tiller steering the ship. He stood up and smiled a half smile at Curtis and said "I'm glad to be going into a war with these men, each one would give their life for the man next to them" Curtis heard John but said nothing, he just starred at the direction he was steering. In Curtis's mind he was thinking of what John had said. Curtis felt eerie with these words, for he knew that when battle is upon them that men who seem loyal sometimes run in the face of danger. Curtis had seen these kinds of cowards before and was not too eager to award anyone the kind of credit that John had. Some of these men he had fought with before, but not many. Curtis was a young man in his last battle. Most of the soldiers he fought with back then were dead or dying.

The men slowly woke up and began to row. The ships were lined up side by side with a ten yard gap between them. A few were leaking so profusely that some soldiers only jobs were to take helmets and use them as buckets to cast the water over the side. The only thing any of the men could see on either sides of the ship was water. They were moving at a good speed but no sign of land was anywhere to be found. The seagulls were gone now and the only types of animals around were the horses. The sea was calm and the water was undisturbed.

Two days had passed like this and the horses were restless as well as the men. John looked to the old fisherman and asked "How many more days to Aodhan?" the old man turned to John and said "Aodhan? Thought you wanted to go to the Kingdom of Dolg" he laughed and turned away from John saying "We will get there soon enough young King, soon enough" John turned to Aaron and whispered "This old fisherman is going to take us in circles. He probably hasn't been to Aodhan in seventy years" Aaron scoffed and whispered back "I think you're exaggerating. It's probably been more like ninety" the old fisherman turned to both of them and said "It's been fifteen years since I last saw Aodhan. By the way my hearing is as good as it was ninety years ago" John and Aaron looked at each other in embarrassment and both sat down.

It was now the fifth day and the old fisherman turned to John and said "I was afraid that might happen" John walked over to him and said "What do you mean" "That storm way out there. Storms like that stir up creatures and tear apart ships" the fisherman said while shaking his head in worry. John looked out at the Sea and said "I don't see anything. Are you sure old man?" "I'm sure. Tie down everything that can't swim. It's going to be a long night" he replied. John passed the word through the ranks and every ship began to secure the loose items. Then they sat still waiting for the storm to arrive. Just as the sun was setting a few light sprinkles of water began to fall from the sky. The men were rowing the ships and preparing for what the old fisherman had warned them about.

Two hours had passed in the night and no more than a few light showers had occurred. The waves had picked up slightly but by no means did they pose a threat. Some of the soldiers began to laugh and joke about the old man's prediction. John even smiled at some of the mockery. Then all of a sudden lightning so bright that it lit up the entire sky struck down from the heavens and into the water. Following the lightning was a monstrous boom of thunder. The horses began calling out in a frantic panic. Even the soldiers had stopped rowing and looked to the sky.

The insult to the old fisherman ceased instantly and all eyes were on him. He looked back at the men and said "What? You thought it would be a pony ride getting here? I told you, now just wait. This is only the beginning" John looked at his Captains and said "Get ready, this trip might end quicker than we expected" just then another crash of lightning and a louder quake of thunder sounded. The rain began right after, pouring fiercely. The waves jumped over the front of the ships and came down on the soldiers like a whip. This was the storm the old man spoke of. Now it was serious and the men knew their mocking comments had come back to bite them.

The men continued to row and the helms men continued to steer. John stood in the middle of his ship praising his men for their courage. "Keep rowing men of Carraig! We go to battle to defend the innocent and protect our home land! You are the heart and soul of our Kingdom" he said proudly while the men looked at him with confidence. They felt their souls awaken with his powerful words and looked on towards the dark with valor in their eyes. Then a loud high pitched shriek was heard from all around. "That's the whales coming up to the surface to feed on the electric eels. They like the way they tickle their tongues" the old man laughed as he looked in the horrified eyes of some of the younger soldiers around him. "Did you think the war in Aodhan would be difficult? Getting to Aodhan is the hard part. Good thing it's the nice time of year to travel by Sea" the old man laughed out again.

The shrieks continued and so did the lightning and thunder. The waves grew with each passing second and the wind was picking up. John looked up just in time to see a gigantic dark figure fly out of the water only thirty yards in front of his ship. It was a whale, its size was as long and wide as the ship John was in. It came back down in the water with a splash so high it rocked John's ship from side to side. "Will it attack us?" John asked the old fisherman. "No, no, they don't bother the ships. It's the giant white sharks that will bite through a ship. They come to eat the whales and sometimes mistake ships for them" the old fisherman said with no humor in his voice this time. John sat down, soaked in salt water. He began to question his decision on making this quest across the Sea of Arrachtaigh.

The men in all the ships old and young continued to row in hopes of reaching safer water. Their hopes dwindled down by every passing hour. The waves kept crashing into the ships. Some men rowing had water up to their knees. The soldiers couldn't keep up with throwing the water over the sides. More and more water was coming in. The ships were now fifty to sixty yards apart and some were losing sight of the lead ship with the old fisherman as the guide. The ships had lanterns lit so the others farther away could still follow but they continued to go out and John feared he might lose some of his men forever.

One ship began to sink. It had taken on so much water the men could not save it. It slowly sank into the abyss. The soldiers from that ship began to swim to another ship nearly seventy yards away. The horses tried swimming but were swallowed up by the waves. One horse appeared as if it would make it to the nearby ship but with only fifteen more yards to go; an enormous white shark leapt out of the cold deep water grabbing it and took it under.

Ten men reached the nearby ship and were quickly pulled aboard. The others were never seen again. John had no knowledge of any of this going on. His ship too was leaking and he began to toss water over the side with his helmet. Lightning struck and lit up the sky again. As John looked in his helmet he saw that what he had was not water but thick red blood. He poured it out over the side and looked over the edge of the ship waiting for the lightning to strike again. When it did he saw a horrific sight. The top of the water was covered with blood.

A dark shadow could be seen in the distance. John ordered his men to sail close to it. He thought perhaps it was another ship or a boat dead in the water. As they began to pass this object John realized it was dead in the water but it was no ship. The dark shadow floating on the top of the water was the carcass of a giant whale. This is where the blood had come from. The blood had left a trail through the water and had entered through the leaking ships.

"Just as I had feared. The white sharks have come" the old fisherman said to John. "We must row faster! Hurry men! Row! Row! Row! " John yelled with strength in his command. "We are not dying here today!" he continued to say. Just then a huge wave began to climb in front of them. It grew and grew thirty feet high. All the men in all of the ships were rowing as fast and hard as they could to climb this mountain of a wave.

A loud cracking sound echoed in the dark. It was a ship breaking apart while trying to scale the massive wave. Men began to scream as they were flung into the Sea. The other ships could here this and continued to row in hopes of not falling into the same fate as their now lost comrades. John did not have time to mourn his fallen soldiers for he was now concerned with his own life. His ship reached the top of the wave and darted down the other side. The rain was pounding the ships as they crossed over the top of the massive wave. Only one ship was too far behind to reach the top and cross over to safety. The wave came crashing down on the top of that ship and killed all who were aboard.

Just as John was beginning to lose hope of making it out of this storm alive, the rain stopped. The waves died down and the lightning was a mere flash of light far away from where he was. John and his men looked ahead and could see little glimpses of light. John thought these were lanterns from ships maybe only a few miles away. As his ship got closer he could make out the shadow of what appeared to be a coastline. The light he saw was coming from lanterns and camp fires near some tents. These tents were out in front of a large castle. They had made it to Aodhan and were coming up on the shores in front of the Castle of Alexander.

CHAPTER VI

THE PEOPLE OF AODHAN

The ships came in slowly and cautious. The men of Carraig didn't know if the Castle of Alexander had been taken over. They also took into consideration that they might be mistaken for the enemy. As they rowed the ships only twenty yards from the coast John yelled out at the top of his lungs "People of Aodhan! It is I, King John from the North Capital of Carraig!" a minute went by and there was no answer. John looked at Curtis as he drew his sword. "Well, should we beach the ships and walk into their camp?" John asked his Captains. Curtis replied in a low whisper "It could be a trap. The whole thing could have been a trap" just then a voice in the dark hollered out to the ships "Welcome men of Carraig! I am King Adeen of Aodhan! I will send men down to the beach to help pull your ships on shore!"

John signaled with his hand for Curtis to beach the ships. "Well old man you got us here and for that I am very grateful" John said to the old fisherman as he placed his sword back in its sheath. One by one the ships landed on the shore. They dropped the front ramps and led the horses out. Men from Aodhan came down with ropes and dragged the ships on shore. King Adeen walked to John and held out his hand, John extended his and the two kings met for the first time. "Thank you for coming and hearing my plea for help" Adeen said to John with happiness in his voice. "My people were ambushed in the night by these heathens. They spared no one except a few they made into slaves. Make camp and at first light we shall discuss any plans you might have" Adeen said. "I will see you at first light" John replied back.

Adeen had been King of Aodhan for many years. He had seen many battles. However, now he was old and unable to wield a sword. He was a nice man but the war would have to be led by John and his Captains. The soldiers from Aodhan were few in number but the few that were there looked fearsome with anger pouring out of their souls. The soldiers left in Aodhan were the survivors from the first battle and wanted revenge on the men who killed their families. They would follow John to either death or victory.

In the distance John heard two dogs barking. They reminded him of his dogs he had left back in the North Capital to protect Elaine. This was the first time he had thought of her since he had left Carraig. This was the longest he had been from her and his heart started to ache for her and his family. He looked up and started heading up the beach towards the castle when he heard a man say "Sire, I think the dogs down at the ship I came on are yours. They jumped aboard our ship when we were pulling off the shore at North Harbor" John turned around quickly and said "Show me" the man hurried down the beach with John closely behind him. When they approached the ship John called out "Roman, Cain" then to John's amazement both Roman and Cain rounded the corner and ran to his feet. They were still dressed in their battle attire. John was more than excited to see them. He thanked the soldier for finding him and showing him to his old friends. John then made his way up the beach to the base of the castle. King Adeen had tents set up for the soldiers of Carraig.

John shared a tent with his Captains and his dogs. They set patrols along the perimeter of Alexander. They also placed guards around the tents. Curtis had his archers in one area of the camp and Simon had his stables and riders in another area. The rest were foot soldiers and made up the rest of the camp. John's tent was in the very center. The men finally slept good being on solid ground. However, a small few of them were unable to cope with the rock of the sea, and now back on land they continued to sway back and forth. After awhile even they too fell asleep and regained their composure.

The next morning every man was awake and ready for battle when the sun rose onto the Woods of Dyr where the Castle of Alexander rest. There were women serving eggs and bread to all of the soldiers while John and Adeen discussed the plans of an attack. "I will send my riders south through the plains of Gronn and my archers east of the Woods of Dyr. Once my archers have made it far enough east they will turn south all the way through Gronn and set up along the edge of the Woods of Stillhet. I will travel south with the rest of the foot soldiers up to the Castle of Aodhan. Once we have them surrounded and the only place for them to go is more south right into the Sea; I will send out a messenger and offer peace if they leave and never return. If they refuse, we attack" John presented to Adeen. Adeen was confident with Johns approach. "The lives of my people are in your hands. Go and send these outcast back into the Sea of Dtonnta Arda" Adeen said with malice in his voice. "Leave what is left of your army here to protect you should the worst happen" John said in a confident manner. Without any hesitation, Adeen nodded his head in approval and acceptance. To Adeen, this was a gesture of John's goodwill. However, to John, this was a means to keep any problems from arising between his men and the men of Aodhan. If they were this badly beaten by the enemy in their home land; how could he put his faith in them now? John trusted his men with his life but he knew nothing of these men. When Adeen agreed to keep his men at the Castle of Alexander; this put John's mind a little more at ease.

John informed his Captains of the plan. Simon began to assemble his riders and prepared to move out. Curtis did the same with his archers and Aaron gathered the foot soldiers who would travel with King John. Aaron smiled at the men when they walked past to get in the marching lines "It's a good day to die" he said while laughing. War to him was more of a game, a game where death is always the victor. Simon was riding by and spotted John with his dogs a few feet from Aaron. "King John" Simon called out. John turned and looked at him. "Yes Captain" he replied. "I'll see you on the battle field. May your sword swing strong like your fathers" Simon said with honor. "Yours as well my friend" replied John with assurance.

Simon reared up his horse and headed towards his men. Just then Curtis walked up behind John. He was holding something that looked like a blanket. John felt someone standing behind him so he turned slowly to see who it was. He saw it was Curtis and asked "What's that you carry?" Curtis looked John in the eyes and said "I brought this from Carraig. This is your fathers bear skin. He would wear it into battle, I'm sure you remember the stories" John looked at this heirloom of his fathers and slowly reached his hand out for it while saying "Yes, I remember the stories" Curtis smiled and said "Well, it's still a little damp from the ride over but I figured this was as good a time as any to award you with it" John smiled back and thanked Curtis for taking the time to find this item. Curtis nodded his head at John and Aaron then walked to his archers.

Simon and his riders headed out on the path south towards the Castle of Aodhan. Curtis and his archers did the same towards the east. John and Aaron led the march south. The footsteps of the soldiers could be heard from nearly a mile away. This was ok in John's eyes; he wanted the enemy to know he was coming. He wanted them to hear cold steel banging together with a great host of men carrying it. He wanted his enemy to fear the unknown that approached; the unknown that brought with them vengeance and turmoil. John looked forward with a stern face as he rode down the path. His mind raced with anxiety and curiosity. He too was traveling to the unknown but his excitement at this point outweighed his fear. His fear of defeat, his fear of losing his family, and his fear of disappointing his father were gone. He had one goal and that was to meet the ice cold sting of battle.

About a mile from Alexander John spotted someone walking along the tree line. John sent three soldiers to escort the man to him. When the soldiers returned with the man John recognized him immediately. It was one of his scouts they had sent over with the messenger from Aodhan. "Report" John said eagerly. "Sire, three camps. One is four miles east of the Castle of Aodhan. Another is on the south shore where the enemy's ships are beached and the main camp is at the castle itself" replied the scout. John looked at him from a top his horse and said "Good work, where are the other scouts?" the scout shook his head and replied with "I lost sight of them a few days ago". John nodded at him and the scout got into the back of the marching line. A soldier looked over at the scout and asked "what are the enemy soldiers like?" the scout glanced back at the soldier and whispered "they are not to be underestimated, that is for sure". The other soldiers around were looking closely at the scout wanting more information. Once the scout noticed this he turned to them and said "They are big and very strong but they lack skill and talent with their weapons" this put the few soldiers who were concerned minds at ease somewhat. A few of the seasoned soldiers that heard this scoffed and looked forward with their unwavering stares.

John only had five horses with him. He and Aaron rode two and the other three were being used to haul weapons, water, and food. John called out for the scout and he quickly returned back to the front "Here sire" he said. "I need you to take one of the horses and ride east. Find Curtis and tell him we meet a mile north of the enemy's eastern camp" John said in a rushed voice. The scout was a short scrawny soldier who could hide easily. He took off the gear from one of the horses and headed east. John looked at Aaron and said "We will attack the camp east of the Castle of Aodhan first. Simon will wait for us to arrive before he attacks. I can't spare anymore horses to inform him of our plans". Aaron looked at John with approval and said "Simon's going to be upset when we have the first battle". John laughed and replied with "Only if we win the first battle, will he ever know".

John and his men began to head southeast to hold up in front of the enemy camp and wait for Curtis. Curtis and his archers were having a hard time making it through the dense forest. Curtis was a big man and his weapons continuously were being snagged on tree limbs and bushes. He told his men "Pick up the pace or the war will be over before we get there". His men hurried as fast as they could manage, they didn't want to anger their Captain. They looked up to Curtis and did not want to disappoint his lust for battle. Curtis had always been good to his men and in return they gave him every possible effort they could in any instance that was required of them. Curtis knew this and cherished the lives and comfort of his men; their safety and well being was top of his priority, other than serving his king.

Simon and his riders came across a few men who were riding towards Alexander. They claimed that they had heard word for all able body's of Aodhan to meet for the war. Simon confirmed this and offered them a place amongst him and his men. They accepted and offered to act as guides for they were born and raised in this land and new every square inch. Simon was a humble man and gladly took their help. After a few hours on the road talking with these men Simon found out they were brothers named Han and Edmond. Their family had been killed on the first raid by the enemy and they were surviving in the wild. Simon also found out that both men were excellent hunters and trackers. He felt that both of these men would come in to great use during this campaign. They continued to make their way south through the Woods of Dyr. After a full days ride Simon and his men made it to the border where the Woods of Dyr become the Plains of Gronn. Simon told his men to make camp for the night. Guards were posted at all four points of the camp and walking sentries were given assigned sectors. Fires were ordered to be kept low and voices as well. The horses had plenty of grass now that they had reached the plains. There was also a fresh water stream that crossed through their camp. The men quietly rested in hopes of finding the enemy the next day.

John and his men had not made it as far. They too were making camp and setting up the necessary security precautions. Roman had caught a rabbit on the march down and was devouring it while John's other dog Cain watched and begged. Finally once Roman had nearly finished it completely he allowed Cain the remaining few pieces. John was sitting at a small fire next to Aaron watching his dogs. Aaron had fallen asleep sitting up next to a log he had rolled over to the fire. His chin was bobbing up and down off of his stocky chest. John looked at him and gave a small laugh. He then focused his mind on Elaine. John now began to miss her more than ever. He pictured times that they had shared together and smiled at the thought. He slowly fell asleep with the image of her smiling back at him in his mind.

Curtis and his archers were not so fortunate. They not only had to make up time for traveling many miles east before bearing down south; they too had to make up time for traveling so slowly through the woods. Curtis and his men were the only group that didn't have the convenience of a road or already made path. Curtis told his men that they would make camp in a few more miles. They were still six miles north of John and eleven miles northeast of Simon.

Curtis noticed a light up ahead through some trees. It was a small fire and several voices could be heard. Curtis motioned with his hand for his men to stop moving. One of his archers stepped up to Curtis and said "Captain, should I go scout ahead?" Curtis whispered back to him "Take three men and circle them, I will enter their camp and determine if they are friend or foe". The rugged looking archer with long black hair and a long black beard slowly made his way around the back of the fire with his bow in hand. Three other soldiers accompanied him and surrounded the men at the fire. Curtis crept up close to the fire to get a look at these men. He noticed they were wearing clothing that didn't match any of the men he had seen from Aodhan. They also didn't have the same style of weapons the soldiers from Aodhan carried.

Curtis waited and listened to them talk. One of them was saying he wanted more wine and another replied back with "You shouldn't have drunk all of it last night. When we find out where the last of the Aodhan soldiers are hiding we can report back to Lord Calder and he will surely reward us with more wine". When Curtis heard this he knew these men were scouts from the enemy side. Curtis drew his sword and leaped out from behind the bush he was hiding. With one swing he beheaded the man who had wanted more wine. He then turned around swiftly and did the same to the man who had spoken of their plans to find the men of Aodhan. Another man stood up and reached for his sword but before he could pull it out he was stuck with four arrows,

all of which pierced his heart. The first arrow was shot by
the rugged looking archer Curtis had ordered to surround
the camp.

Curtis looked at him as he walked through the bushes
and said "Good work Amnon" "Now grab what you can
from them and put out the fire. We need to keep moving"
Amnon and the other three archers collected a few weapons
and gold from the dead men and buried the fire. Then
Curtis and the rest of the archers continued south for two
more hours in the dark. They finally reached a point where
Curtis gave the order to make camp and sleep. Curtis told
his men no fires; there may be more enemy scouts. It was
the beginning of summer and the end of spring; nights in
Aodhan were warm. Curtis had finally got to kill the enemy
and he smiled as he slept, dreaming of battle. Curtis had
been the first man of Carraig to kill the enemy. This was a
great honor and would surely be recognized in the history
of Carraig. The other archers looked up to Curtis even more
now and they all longed for the next shot from their bow
that would deem them worthy of being in the company of
the mighty Captain of Carraig, Curtis. Amnon too had shot
the enemy and would be recognized for this. He is Curtis
right hand man and has been for many years. Amnon is a
skilled warrior and an excellent bow man. He and Curtis
have had many shooting tournaments against one another
and Amnon never lost by much.

CHAPTER VII

THE PATH TO WAR

The next morning John and his men made their way southeast. Aaron in a curious voice looked over at John riding his horse and asked "So I guess we aren't going to ask if they want to leave Aodhan in exchange for peace?" John looked at Aaron for a brief moment and then back at the road ahead while saying "We are going to ask them when we get to the Castle of Aodhan" Aaron looked confused and asked "I thought we were going to attack an enemy camp first?" John replied with a stern look on his face "We are going to destroy this enemy camp. After, we will offer the enemy held up in the castle peace. If they choose it we will allow them to leave but I will not let an enemy camp flank us from the east" Aaron looked back with a smile and said "Oh good, I would have hated to come all this way and not get to enjoy at least one little battle". John wasn't amused at this talk of killing he wanted to be back with Elaine and his boys. In the back of his mind he wanted to turn around and go home. Then he would think of the safety of his people and he marched on with his war mind set again.

The afternoon came and John and his men reached the edge of Dyr and the beginning of Gronn. They rested shortly and then pressed on. After a few miles through the plains John spotted a house. There were two horses out front. John sent a few men to investigate. The men came back with a boy around thirteen years old. John asked the boy where his parents were. The boy told him that his mother had died when he was younger and his father went to Alexander to join with the soldiers. The boy told John he was taking care of the farm until his father returned. John clarified his position with the boy and let him go back to his home. John looked at Aaron and told him they were only a day's walk from the next border. The Woods of Stillhet are where they will meet Curtis.

John and his men continued to march. Meanwhile, Simon and his riders were nearly at the west border of Gronn and Stillhet. Simon asked Han "How far is the Castle of Aodhan once we reach the border?" Han replied with "Only a few miles. I can take us to a spot where we can see the castle and still be far enough away where we don't have to worry about being spotted by the enemy" "Good, very good" Simon said with a smile of animosity. Simon and his riders sustained their pace towards the border. Little did they know that Curtis had already taken out two enemy soldiers; Simon and his riders bragged about which one of them would get the first kill out of this war. Simon with a smirk on his face listened to all of the boasting. Then with a cool and calm voice he simply said "all of you think you will get the first strike on the enemy, but I lead the way into the battle" he said this while sitting tall on his horse and looking forward. His men stopped their comments and smiled towards their leader as if they truly knew; if there would be a first kill, then it would surely be from Simon's doing. Simon was also given much respect from his men. Many of them longed for his acceptance and hoped to be as great as he one day.

Curtis and his men reached the Plains of Gronn. They hurried along a small river that flowed south. The archers were moving quickly with their minds ready for war. Because their leader had already slain two of the enemy they were impatient to do the same. "We must keep our speed. King John and his men are most likely well ahead of us by now" Curtis hollered to his men. Curtis was still under the impression that he was going to flank the Castle of Aodhan. He didn't know that he was in route straight for an enemy camp that John planned to ambush. The scraggly messenger that John had sent out never found Curtis. He became lost and wondered the wild for weeks before returning to Alexander in shame.

Over in the west, Simon and his men were crossing into the Woods of Stillhet. They followed Han's lead in the forest. They continued on the road for a half mile then Han turned off the path and into the wilderness. Simon was uncertain if the horses would be able to make it to the place Han spoke of. Then after what seemed like an hour they came to a clearing. Simon looked around and said to Han "This is a perfect place to set up a camp but I don't see the castle" Han climbed down from his horse and said to Simon "Follow me this way" Simon got off his horse and followed Han. They came to a small cliff where the clearing ended and the trees began again. "Look through those trees" Han said while pointing off the cliff. Simon leaned over and peered out. He could see everything from there. He could see the Castle of Aodhan and miles in either direction. Simon could even see the Sea. It wasn't clear enough to see where the ships that the enemy had sailed in on were but it was still a perfect location.

Simon congratulated Han and Edmond for leading them there. He then ordered a perimeter set with walking sentries. Simon had a soldier watching through the trees down at the castle. "If you see any movement let me know immediately" Simon said to the lookout. Then they set up a camp and prepared to wait for a sign of King John and his men. It would only take them thirty minutes to reach the castle from where they were. Simon was getting anxious for this war to really start. He could look down and see the smoke from the enemy camps. He knew it was only a matter of time before he would be riding at a full gallop into a line of enemy soldiers. The sun was beginning to go down and Simon told his men to eat and try to rest. His riders were ready for war more than ever now. It was hard for most of them to sleep. Thoughts of battle kept them awake.

John and his men had been marching since sun up and now with the sun just going down they reached the border of Stillhet. They had passed several villages on their way down. Most of the men from these villages were too old to fight and the few that were capable were in Alexander guarding King Adeen. John told his men to make camp for the night. John also gave the order for no fires. They were too close to enemy territory to risk being spotted in the dark. Now John and his men would wait here until Curtis and his archers arrive.

John gave the order to armor down. The men were allowed to take off their armor as long as it was in close proximity to where they could dawn it if necessary.

Again Curtis and his archers traveled at night. Their footsteps were silent as they moved across the Plains of Gronn. Curtis and his men were beginning to feel groggy. All of them were sleep deprived and had been going at a continuous fast pace. Still Curtis pushed forward. After traveling many hours into the night Curtis gave the order to set up camp. The men fell asleep almost instantly. Three hours later the sun was up and beating down on them. The men covered their tracks and began their move south again. Curtis could see the tree line only a few miles away. One of John's soldiers spotted something in the distance but couldn't clearly make out if it was an animal or a man. He went to Aaron and told him of the sighting. Aaron sent a few scouts to confirm what the soldier had seen. Within thirty minutes the scouts returned to Aaron with news that Curtis and his archers were nearly on their location. Aaron went to John and told him of the news. John got on his horse and rode out to meet Curtis who was only a few hundred yards away now.

Curtis looked out and saw a rider closing in on him and his men. He spread out his archers in case it was an enemy spy. With a closer look Curtis saw that the rider was wearing a bear skin as a cloak and he instantly new it was John. Curtis yelled to his men "It's the King! Hurry, let's go!" Curtis ran towards John. Curtis was confused. Why was King John this far east and alone? He thought to himself while he ran like a rabid dog with his men close behind him. When he reached John he looked in his eyes for answers.

John immediately spoke out to the men "There is an enemy camp only a few miles south of here. Curtis, take your men east around their camp and prepare for the attack" without hesitation Curtis continued his stride southeast into the Woods of Stillhet. John rode back to his men and put them in battle formation. A scout led John through the woods to the enemy camp. The plans had changed and now John wanted everyone quite. The men held their weapons tight to prevent them from clanging.

Curtis and his archers found the enemy camp. They were loud and easy to track. Curtis had five hundred archers at his command and positioned them around the entire east flank. Amnon was in charge of the left side while Curtis commanded the right. It was great positioning for the archers. They came as close as twenty feet away from the enemy concealed behind tall trees and thick bushes. Now they were just waiting on John and his foot soldiers to start the attack.

John and his men were closing in on the camp. John took seven hundred and fifty men to the north of the camp. Aaron took another seven hundred and fifty to the west of the camp. It was completely surrounded by John's men. The only escape for the enemy would be to the south and into the Sea. This enemy camp was too far east to be able to make it to the ships they sailed in on. If they ran then John would run them into the Sea and their doom would be a watery grave. John and his soldiers came only one hundred yards away when John noticed this camp had more men than he expected. It was an entire army of at least a thousand men.

John took a deep breath and let it out. He was ready for this battle. It was going to be the perfect surprise attack.

John had trained for battle his whole life and this is what it had come down to. He thought of Elaine and his boys. Then looked up and said out loud in a soft voice "Father, look down on me". John held his head high and grasped his sword with his right hand and slowly unsheathed it. With a roaring voice he yelled "Attack!" every man in John's army heard his command and ran forward towards the enemy camp with their weapons drawn.

The enemy soldiers heard John and his men running full speed at them. They began yelling out "Ambush!" over and over while attempting to gain their weapons. Some already had swords attached at their waist. Those men ran to the front line to meet John and his men head on. John was the first to make contact with the enemy. He swung his sword and struck a man killing him instantly. The rest of the foot soldiers engaged the enemy and the battle began.

Curtis and his archers were dropping enemy soldiers like flies. Arrow's filled the camp; they pierced over two hundred men in a matter of minutes. John climbed down from his horse and began fighting on the ground; he preferred this over fighting from horseback. John continued to swing over and over again. With every swipe of his sword he sliced through enemy flesh. His once bright blade was now dark red with the blood of his enemies. John now knew what battle was really like. This was not a story his father had told him. He could hear the screams of men as they lay dying on the ground. This part he did not enjoy but the taste of victory overwhelmed his eyes and he continued to tear through the enemy one at a time.

The enemy's numbers were dwindling down and Curtis left his concealed location and drew his sword. He wanted to fight the enemy closer than with a bow and arrow. Curtis found John on the battle ground and came up beside him. Curtis hollered to John "This is how I used to fight with your father. Side by side" John looked at him with a face dripping with blood splatter and yelled back "I'm glad you're with me now old friend".

Just then, the biggest soldier of the enemy's army was face to face with Curtis. Two more came around a tent and ran towards John. Curtis exchanged blows back and forth with this giant of a man. Curtis took a stab wound to the shoulder and yelled out in pain and anger. John heard Curtis and tried to make his way to him. John sliced through one of the enemy's chest and he fell with a thud. Then he went for the other missing his target and striking the ground. As the enemy soldier's sword was coming down on John's back Aaron came out of nowhere and decapitated this foe. John stood up and turned towards Curtis just in time to see Curtis plunge his sword deep into the belly of the enemy warrior. John looked back at Aaron but Aaron was already off to another enemy soldier. John regained his feet and took off towards Aaron's location. Curtis grabbed at his shoulder and began to jog after John. The three swung left and right at the enemy; striking them down together and watching after one another.

Roman and Cain could be heard in the distance. For their first time in battle they were doing very well. The two dogs had assisted in thirty kills. Roman had a huge dent on his armor where he had been struck with an axe. Cain had blood on his armor that was not his own. They were both physically sound. Together they made a deadly pair. It was not hard for the dogs to determine who the enemy was. The difference in clothing and armor were enough but they also could tell by the fear in the enemy's eyes when they gazed at the massive pair. John's men had been around the dogs for a long time and knew how to maneuver around them. Many of the enemy soldiers would run in horror when they saw them.

The enemy camp was now painted red. It was lined with the bodies of fallen soldiers from both sides. What remained of the enemy army ran into the trees to the south were Amnon was waiting with two hundred archers. They shot their arrows straight and true killing the last of these pillaging villains. This battle was over and King John was victorious.

John ordered for a body count of his men. Within an hour he found out that one hundred of his foot soldiers and two archers had given their lives for this noble cause. John had their bodies burnt on top of a mound. He then had the bodies of the enemy piled on top of each other in the center of their camp. They too he had burnt.

Curtis gathered his men as did Aaron and they began to march for the Castle of Aodhan. This battle had been won but the war was far from over. Curtis led the way in front of John and the rest of the foot soldiers. From time to time they would come across a few enemy soldiers in transit from the castle to what they thought was their camp to the east. Curtis took the pleasure in ending their lives.

A few hours into their march west one of the men from Aodhan that had been picked up from a village informed John that they were only a few miles from the castle. John ordered that they set up camp and told his men to rest because the next battle would be in the morning. Curtis and his archers spread out in a hundred yard radius of the camp in case they had enemy visitors. There was a stream nearby this camp where the men washed the blood off of themselves and their clothing. Many men had minor wounds and cleaned them. The rest of the men sharpened their weapons. John let the men have small fires and they cooked a few deer that the archers had shot down earlier. The men's nerves had settled down now that the first battle had come to an end.

After nightfall most of John's camp slept. Except John, his mind was on the battle. He would have been killed if Aaron hadn't of been there. John thought of Elaine and what she might say if she had been there to see. He looked over at Aaron and saw him starring back with one eye open. "Thanks for saving me earlier" he said to Aaron in a humble voice. "I saved you? Oh yeah well just doing my duty to the King" Aaron said in a clever voice. "You know what I'm talking about" John said with a smirk. Aaron replied with "I just saw you and Curtis fighting together and didn't want to be left out. You killed one and I knew Curtis was going to kill the giant; I figured if I didn't whack that one's head off that was on top of you I'd never hear the end of it" Aaron said with a serious face. John laughed while looking at Aaron. Aaron continued with his serious face then rolled over and went to sleep. John shook his head with a smile and closed his eyes.

To the far west Simon and his men were beginning to wonder where John and his men were. "They should have been here a day ago" Simon said to one of his riders. Han over heard and said "Give them another day. Your King is not used to the terrain and his men are on foot. If they don't come by tomorrow I will ride out and find them" Simon looked at Han and nodded his head. He still felt they should have made it to the clearing in front of the castle. This kept him up for many hours into the night. Finally, shortly after midnight Simon fell asleep.

When morning came around, Simon was up and over with the lookout. "Any sign of the King?" he asked the soldier on watch. "No sign of the King, but more enemy soldiers just arrived at the castle from the south and are setting up tents" the watchman explained. "How many did you count? Simon asked. With a hesitant reply the watchman said "Five hundred. Maybe more" Simon shook his head and said out loud to himself "Where are you John?" Han was on his horse and rode up to Simon and asked "Shall I go scout around for the rest of your people?" Simon looked up at his stone cold face and said "Wait until noon, if there is no sign of them ride out".

Just then the watchman came up to Simon and said in a relieved voice "I've spotted them; a thousand or so men are marching up to the castle. They are about a mile out. Another five hundred are circling the eastside of the castle. We must ride down from the west for a flanking position" Simon looked at him with a smile and yelled out to all of his riders "Mount up! We ride to the King's aide!" with that, all five hundred men climbed upon their horses and formed a line with four abreast. The first four were Simon in the middle and Han and his brother to the left of Simon. Simons second in command Aral was to his right. When the camp was packed and all the riders in line, they began to ride down the hillside to close in on the enemy's camp.

The enemy had also seen John's army closing in and a massive bell began to ring. All of the enemy troops began to scramble to their fighting positions. This enemy bell could be heard all the way south to the enemy ships. Those men began to gather their weapons and prepare to march towards the castle. It would take them at least an hour to reach the castle, with around three hundred men.

John and his army had begun their march towards the castle a few hours before sun up to arrive for battle just as the enemy was rising out of their tents. Curtis and his archers were in range to the east and John with Aaron were only a half mile from the castle when they all looked to the west to see Simon and his riders flying down a hillside to the west. "Right on time" John said to Aaron while pointing his finger at the riders. "It's about time they got involved in this war" Aaron said with smirk.

The enemy soldiers set up a wall of men outside of the Castle of Aodhan. They had archers of their own on top of the castle walls above the enemy troops. The enemy Lord Calder was on top of the castle wall looking right at John; who was covered in his father's bear skin. John sat on top of his horse looking straight back with vicious eyes. The two couldn't see one another well enough to make out any physical features but they both new each other were the leaders of each army.

John gave the signal for the messenger to ride out to the enemy Lord and offer the terms of their return home for peace. Also the messenger was to alert the enemy Lord of the demise of his enemy camp to the east. As the messenger approached the castle he saw the bodies of the scouts that had been sent over with the messenger from Aodhan. All of them were hanging upside down by their feet off the castle wall; while crows picked at their faces. They had been dead for a week.

Calder heard the terms John had offered and was not pleased. He was curious to why the men of Carraig had come so far on behalf of Adeen. Calder who was nearly seven feet tall with long thick blonde hair and nearly as long of a beard to match; started laughing at the messenger. Calder said "Your King will die today messenger, along with every man here. Give this message to your King" a single arrow had been fired from one of the enemy archers piercing the messengers shoulder. The messenger turned his horse around and rode hard back to John.

John saw this and immediately ordered the charge. Over one thousand soldiers from the North of Carraig ran towards the castle with their swords, spears, and axes drawn. Curtis and his archers opened fire from the east. Simon and his well rested riders charged their horses at a full gallop towards the enemy ranks. This battle for the Castle of Aodhan had just begun. The enemy foot soldiers ran out to meet John and his men half way. Battle cries could be heard from both sides as the men ran for each other. Curtis and his men were picking off the enemy one by one as they tried to reach John and his men. Simon and his riders blasted through the west flank of the enemy line mowing them down by the hundreds.

John and his men clashed into the enemy foot soldiers with such a bang it could be heard echoing through the Castle of Aodhan. Roman and Cain went to work picking off enemy soldiers that had been separated from their companies one by one. Aaron was ripping through the adversary's with ease. John was striking down men left and right. The enemy began to call him the bear warrior because they had not yet learned his name. Not one could take John down from his horse. John was quick and his strength struck down his enemies with single blows.

Curtis of course gave up his position as an archer and headed for the closer battle near John and Aaron. He left Amnon in charge of the archers and began to swing an axe in one hand and a sword in the other. He had killed over ten men in a matter of minutes. His face was covered in his enemy's blood and he liked it that way.

Simon was thrown from his horse and began to fight on the ground. Simon had already slain many men with his exceptional skill. One of his riders grabbed his horse and brought it back to him. Simon leaped on his horse and continued to slay his new sworn enemies. Simon's skills were incomparable to any other soldier from any side, he fought with finesse. He was smooth and precise, with every swing of his blade.

John was being admired by the Lord Calder who was still on top of the castle walls. The enemy was being slaughtered in mass amounts. Just then the sound of a horn was being blown from the south. It was over three hundred men from the south who were responding from the enemy's bell that had been rung. John yelled out for all of his men to hear "Reform the line! Enemy soldiers coming from the south" the foot soldiers reformed the lines while still fighting as best they could.

The men from the south attacked John's men with great strength. These men knew how to fight and appeared not to feel pain nor have any fear. They swung their weapons fast and hit their mark nearly every time. John's men started dropping and more and more of the enemy came up from the south shores. The enemy archers were not as accurate as John's archers but they were still killing many men. John was informed of this by Aaron when he looked up with his blood soaked hair and said to John "We might have to call it a day and come back" John looked at his dying men and ordered the retreat.

The men of Carraig began to fall back. Simon yelled out for the men to follow him back to the hillside that was concealed and overlooked the castle. John agreed and the men fled. John was humiliated with his defeat. Even though both sides had lost many men, Calder had managed to come out with the win. He was not cocky but humble for he felt this battle might have ended his rein. Because John was an excellent warrior and his men followed him not only because he was their King but they loved him as a brother.

John and his men climbed the mountain where Simon and the riders had been camping. Once they reached the top, John and his captains sat and ate while discussing their plans of a new attack. After this battle many men had wounds that needed at least a week's healing. John told the men to prepare for an extended stay. The enemy had so many troops; that John couldn't understand it. Where did they all come from? They must have heard of their victories in Aodhan and sent reinforcement troops. This is where all the men had come from. John was sure of it. He figured once Calder discovered his east camp had been destroyed not just the men in it; he would send new men to rebuild it. John knew that he couldn't wait long for his men to heal. They needed to hit the enemy hard again and lower their numbers.

The lookout was back at his post and reported to Simon that the enemy was regrouping and burning the dead. Simon reported this to John. The Captains sat around a small fire and planned the next attack. They would attack with one line of archers in the middle, riders in front of archers, and foot soldiers all around them. It sounded good to John but this battle wouldn't take effect for at least five days while he and his men recovered.

CHAPTER VIII

THE ALLIANCE BETWEEN ADALRIKR

I n the far southeast island where the Kingdom of Adalrikr sets; King Arvid caught word of what his previous Captain, Lord Calder had been doing. The king had allowed his Captain safe passage through the Kingdom of Adalrikr for his services while under Arvid's rule. Calder was a good Captain and fought many battles for King Arvid. However, his actions now reflected poorly on his King. Arvid, now angry with his old friend and comrade for not explaining in detail his true intentions for wanting to retire and travel the land; planned to travel to Aodhan in hopes of ending his cruel raid.

King Arvid does not pity people nor does he show any signs of compassion. None the less, he feared Calder might create enough problems that the other Kingdoms might rally together in the future and come to Adalrikr; searching for Calder and his followers. More and more men began to hear of Calder and view him as a hero who takes what he wants and kills all who deny him. These men gather at the north shores of Adalrikr and sail to Aodhan on a monthly basis to join with Calder on his quest of destruction.

Word of John and his men have not yet reached the shores of Adalrikr. But the overtaking of an entire Kingdom by Lord Calder has. This news went East across Adalrikr to the Black Wood; a place where King Arvid would not dare to go. This is where the "Berserkers" claim refuge. Once there was a great battle between the men of Adalrikr and the Berserkers. Arvid was second in command, while his father King Argen led the attack. More than half of the Kingdom was destroyed by this battle. Argen died from an axe wound wielded by the leader of the Berserker army. Arvid became King instantly and called for a truce between the two. After much more bloodshed the Berserker leader agreed to withdraw his army if the Berserkers be given the Black Wood to the east.

The Black Wood took up one third of the entire Kingdom of Adalrikr. But since Arvid and his men never traveled there anyway he agreed. To this day the Berserkers as well as the people of Adalrikr honor the truce. The Berserkers have not been seen outside the Black Wood since that day. Although, it is said that some of the small village's on the outskirts of Black Wood sometimes trade with the Berserkers.

Arvid sent a single ship to Aodhan with a messenger; to ask Calder to meet with him back in Adalrikr. When the messenger reached the north shore to sail out for Aodhan he was met by a large man with long black hair that was matted together with his beard. The man towered over the messenger and had on a black bear skin for clothing. On his back was a massive axe with a single blade that stretched half the length of the man's body. "I am Grog" the man let out with a growl. "My master wants to speak with your Lord Calder" he said in a demanding way. The messenger looked up into his cold black eyes and replied in a cowering voice "I am just a messenger from King Arvid. But I am on my way to speak with Lord Calder. I…. can tell him for you when I see him". The messenger could clearly tell it was one of the Berserkers he had heard about in stories. Grog looked down at the messenger and said in a low deep voice "I will tell him myself". Grog looked at the messenger as he walked past him and climbed into the ship. The messenger didn't dare to add any comments that were not crucial to the Berserker. He took his seat and motioned for the men to set sail.

Back in Aodhan John's men were beginning to heal from their last battle. John looked through the trees down at the Castle of Aodhan. Calder and his men were regrouped and ready for the next attack. John knew this and everyday he waited to send his men back into battle; Calder would get stronger. "We will ride out at first light" John said to his Captains that were behind him. "I will spread the word throughout the men" Simon replied with a smile on his face. Simon wanted another charge into this enemy. He felt in his heart, this enemy could be beaten in a few days time. He also longed for another chance to prove himself to John and to his men.

Curtis wasn't so optimistic; most likely because he didn't want the war to be over so quickly. "We should attack quickly and leave quickly" Curtis said in a calm voice to John. "If we slowly take out their front lines they will either retreat back to where they came from or surrender" Curtis stated. John sat down near Aaron who was to the left of

Curtis and said "We will see how it goes. If it looks like we can take the castle then we shall". Aaron nodded his head in agreement with John. Just then Simon returned and said "The men know the plan and are ready for dawn". John gave him a quick nod and looked at Aaron and Curtis "Get some rest it's going to be a long day" Aaron looked back at John and said "unless you die right off the charge" John smiled as did the others. It was typical of Aaron to throw out condescending remarks that would gain a smile or even a laugh.

The next morning John and his men slowly crept down the hillside. They were careful not to bang their weapons and armor together. John knew that the enemy would soon be on to them but every second of surprise might mean one less man would have to give his life. When they reached the bottom of the hillside they could see the castle gate clearly. A few of the enemy guards stood watch. At the same time Curtis and Amnon pulled back their arrows and sent them sailing through the air. Both enemy guards were hit through the heart; one fell to his knees while the other fell flat on his back. "Good work" John whispered in the direction of Curtis and Amnon. The foot soldiers began a slow jog towards the castle gate with John and Aaron out in front.

Curtis and Amnon split the archers up into two groups and circled the castle unseen. Simon and his riders also split their ranks into two groups. Simon would lead his group to the east flank and Aral would lead his half all the way around to the west when John gave the signal. Just then a bell began to ring throughout the castle; John had been spotted by a walking sentry from on top of the wall. The gate opened and dozens of enemy soldiers came running out;

they had been waiting for John and his army to arrive. A few hundred archers flooded the top of the wall and opened fire.

Curtis and Amnon's men took down the majority of Calder's archers. Simon led the riders to the front gate of the castle where he continuously struck down his adversary. John and Aaron split up the foot soldiers. John went to the east side of the castle and Aaron took the west. Lord Calder looked on from the high walls of the castle as his men slowly were pushed back. From time to time he would give a signal to shoot a volley from what was left of his archers.

Aaron wielded his axe as the enemy continued to cross his path. He moved quickly around them; striking up and then down on them. His men followed closely as he led right through the middle of the enemy ranks. The ground had been coated with sweat and blood from both sides. Aaron's loud voice could be heard by all as he yelled "We are the men of Carraig and we bring death!" he laughed as he glided through his enemy.

Curtis could hear Aaron and he looked at his archers and gave an order "Don't let up on them. When you see Amnon and his men fall back; fall back with them" he placed his bow around his neck and let it rest across his back. Then he reached to his side were his thick bladed sword had been waiting. He pulled it out quickly and ran towards John and his men. Curtis had a glare on his face as he ran into the battle. Two of the enemy soldiers saw him coming and they both made their charge at him. Curtis jumped in the air and came down hard on the first. His blade struck with so much power the man could not hold on to his sword and it went right into his own chest. Curtis looked at his next victim and smiled while saying "I've never killed a man with his own sword before. Let's see if I can do it again" the enemy soldier looked at Curtis and then turned and ran for his life. Curtis didn't feel like giving chase so he turned and looked for a new opponent. The enemy soldier ran straight into John's blade and in turn ended his own life. John raised his left leg and kicked the coward off of his sword. John turned and continued his charge into the enemy. Not all of Calder's men lacked courage. Some fought bravely and made a fierce challenge to John and his men. Some of these men were just farmers that wanted to join in on the raid. However, others were men from Adalrikr's famous army. These men had fought in multiple battles and were not fearsome of war. John and his men had their work cut out for them when it came down to these warriors.

As more of the enemy came out of the castle Aral led his charge right into them. He was not as skillful as Simon but he had a fierce heart and made up the difference with his speed. He had blonde hair that reached his shoulders and stood at an even six foot tall. Aral was light compared to the other men; only one hundred eighty pounds. When the men would question him, his response was that his older brother, who fought with the foot soldiers, ate all the food when he was younger. His brother Marcus who was close to two hundred and eighty pounds couldn't ride a horse because they kept collapsing from under him over long distance.

Aral saw his brother being attacked across the battlefield by three of Calder's soldiers. He placed his blood stained sword back in its sheath and plucked up a spear that was sticking out of a body on the ground. He charged his solid black mare towards his brother's aggressors. When he came within range he lifted the spear to the side of his head and launched it with great force. Just as his brother swung through one of his enemy's; the other two fell to the ground as well. Aral had thrown his spear through the left side of one man and it had traveled all the way out and into the back of the other. Marcus turned around gasping for breath and nodded up at his brother in thanks. Aral quickly turned his horse around and rode back towards his men. Marcus caught his breath and made his way to the next enemy soldier.

John had been engaging in multiple one on one duel's with the more skilled of Calder's army. He had just struck down one of Calder's Captain's when he heard what sounded like a young boy cry out in pain. As John turned, he saw one of his men that had been shot in the arm by an arrow; fall to the ground. The man crawled backwards on the ground as a much larger man from Calder's army approached him. John recognized the man on the ground. It was the seventeen year old boy who he had met back in Carraig the night the first messenger from Aodhan had come. John moved rapidly to save him. Curtis noticed John running towards something and he hurried to give him aide. As the large man swung down on the boy John threw his sword from ten feet away. It hit the man and prevented him from delivering the fatal blow. He turned towards John and forgot about the boy. John looked around for a weapon but could find none.

As the large man closed in on John the boy made his way to his feet. He picked up John's sword with his good arm and began to run towards John in hopes of rearming his King. John took his fighting stance and was prepared to take on his enemy bare handed. The large man laughed at John's gesture and said "Let us see how the bear warrior holds up against steel" he raised his sword and swung it violently at John. John moved from side to side barely avoiding each blow. Just then Curtis came up behind John and stared in the eyes of the man who was unequally trying to defeat his King. The man locked eyes with Curtis and took a step back. Curtis's rage could be sensed and his battlefield victories could be assumed from his armor soaked in blood and the scars from past enemies. Curtis was not smiling nor laughing such as his previous dealings with this enemy. He was angered at the fact this man thought he was worthy of attacking such a King as John. For that, he would make him pay brutally.

What happened next shocked both Curtis as well as John. The small boy, Harold of merely seventeen years old came from behind the large man and with a mighty swing of King John's sword decapitated him where he stood. Curtis's rage slowly lowered and he looked at the boy "What is your name boy?" Curtis asked in a very intrigued voice. John answered his question as he walked over to reclaim his sword "His name is Harold. Harold of the North Capital" John smiled at the Harold. "Thank you for coming to my aide" John said to him. Harold looked back at John still shaken up from moments earlier but managed to say "Thank you King John but if it hadn't been for you I would already be dead"

John patted him on the shoulder that didn't have an arrow sticking out of it and said "See one of the men to help you get that out and burn it shut" Harold gave an unwilling smile and nodded his head in acknowledgement. Aaron and his men made it over to John's men and they continued to fight. Aaron spotted John and Curtis and made his way over to them hopping over fallen soldiers like a deer. When he arrived in front of John he said "These guys are like ants. You kill one and ten more show up" John looked over at Aaron and reluctantly agreed. "Who's the kid?" Aaron asked. "This is Harold the King saver and giant slayer" Curtis said in an uplifting yet sarcastic voice. John then told Aaron "Have some of your men escort this young man back to the camp and take care of his wound. He did his King a great service and I don't want him injured more before he has time to heal" Aaron looked at Harold with pride and said to him "Follow me young warrior, I'll get you taken care of" Harold followed Aaron towards two of his men that stood much taller than Aaron.

Aaron told them both to look after Harold and make sure he gets back to the camp safely. Both of the men looked down at Harold while saying "Yes Captain" then Aaron took off in a sprint towards some of his men who were fighting outnumbered. As he was running towards them he yelled in a somewhat happy voice "Here I come! Aaron the ant killer!" at one point while jumping over one of his fallen warriors he tripped and fell rolling a few times. He jumped back up and turned from side to side until he spotted his axe. He picked it up and continued his pursuit. Curtis had been watching as well as John. They both looked at each other and smiled while shaking their heads. Once Aaron arrived at his destination he began evening the odds for his men. They watched his enthusiasm and rallied to his side.

The battle lasted five hours and John knew that they would not be able to penetrate the castle walls that day. He yelled out to his men "Pull back! Pull back!" in a disappointed but commanding voice. With that the men fell back and began the hike up the hillside to their camp.

Simon was the last up the hill with his men. Calder called his army back into the castle and sealed the gate. He knew who the victor of this battle was and by no mean was it him. In the back of Calder's mind, he began to question himself to whether or not he should leave now and head home. But he also knew if he did this, he would lose the respect of his countrymen and they would no longer follow him over the seas.

Each Captain including King John had lost about fifty men. The numbers were not comparable to the five hundred of Calder's men that fell on the battle field that day. John and his Captains knew victory was close at hand. John met with his Captains at their now usual spot at the top of the cliff. John congratulated them on a good day's battle. After saying that, he looked at Curtis and said "I want some archers to circle the castle. If any small number of Calder's men leaves the castle, follow them. Do not allow any supplies to be taken to or from the castle". Curtis jumped up and nodded his head.

"Give the men two days to heal and rest. On the morning of the third we attack again" John said while looking at Aaron and Simon. They both agreed and set off to tell the men. This journey was taking longer than John had hoped. He often thought of home but his mind would then stray back to the battle field. He had lost many men already. Most of them were fathers and husbands. John began to feel guilty for their deaths but would shun the idea when he thought of what could happen if Calder made it to Carraig. He knew his brothers along with him would put up a marvelous fight. However, any invasion on his people would lead to the deaths of innocent and peaceful people. He reassured himself of this and kept his spirit high.

Little did John know that in the Castle of Aodhan, Calder was telling his men to pack up and get ready to retreat back to Adalrikr. His numbers had fallen so drastically that he wanted to give up his campaign and return home. Just then one of Calder's men came up to him and said "A ship just pulled in to port from home. It has multiple messengers aboard it, all wanting to speak to you". Calder replied with "send a hundred men to ensure their safe arrival". Within three hours the messengers had reached the castle. Curtis's archers managed to kill several soldiers and wound many more. The messenger from King Arvid spoke first "King Arvid is appalled at the risk you have put Adalrikr in. He demands you withdraw from these lands and immediately meet with him". Calder looked at the messenger and exclaimed "I have suffered a great loss here. Not by Adeen of Aodhan but by King John of Carraig. I plan to return home tomorrow night in the cover of darkness. I will set this castle a blaze and meet with King Arvid". The messenger smiled unknowingly; thinking he would be rewarded for his persuasion skills towards Lord Calder.

Just then the Berserker warrior Grog stormed up to Calder. The two were at eye level but Calder knew he was no man of King Arvid's. Grog looked into Calder's eyes and said "You are not the man I heard about. I heard Calder was a giant of a man and took no prisoners. To think my master wants to join you" Calder's eyes grew with anger yet he was intrigued. He took a step back and began to defend himself "I have lost my warriors! These men of Carraig are young and quick. They fight with the same blood lust that I do.

My men are not trained nor equipped as well as this enemy. I have no choice but to return home and regroup".

Grog looked at him and smirked "My master has given me a message for the mighty pillager Calder" he continued to speak in a sarcastic voice "If you wish to split the spoils of your campaign he will send fifteen hundred Berserker warriors to aide you". Calder looked in amazement that the leader of the Berserkers would make such an offer. Calder looked at Grog and said "Bring the Berserkers. I will hold off John of Carraig until you return. My campaign will continue". Grog nodded his head and with a grunt turned away stomping towards the gate which led back to the ship. The messenger from Arvid came up to Calder and nearly shouted "You said you would meet with King Arvid!" Calder looked over at one of the men that had joined the messenger and said "Will you give a message to Arvid for me?" the man looked back at him and hesitantly said "yes". Calder then looked back at the messenger and pulled his sword making one swish through the air and then placing it back into its sheath. The head of the messenger slowly fell off his lifeless body. Calder picked it up and looked at the man "here is my message" he said while tossing the head to him. The man took the head of the messenger and hurried to the gate. He was riddled with fear and could not speak.

Grog made it back to the ship with the other men he had come with. Calder had lost a few more men while they helped escort them to the port. Grog climbed aboard the vessel and began giving the orders. They immediately set sail back towards Adalrikr. Grog grabbed an ore and began to help row in an attempt to get back to his leader faster and deliver the news. None of the men on the ship questioned his authority. They continued to row at his fast pace without daring to stop. Grog ordered the men to row nonstop to the north port of Adalrikr. If a man would fall asleep, Grog would give a loud growl "Wake up!" The wind helped push them along and they made record time cutting through the Sea. The men hurried to grab a drink or shove a piece of bread in their tired and hungry mouths. They did this when Grog would go to the front of the ship and take a look around.

Back in John's camp the men rested, healed, and began to regain their strength. Simon had his two new friends Han and Edmond go out and hunt for food for the entire camp. They would return every few hours with a new kill. They would either bring back elk, deer, rabbits, or sometimes a few large squirrels. The two brothers specialized in hunting and this was an easy task assigned to them that they enjoyed. Simon also had a few of his men go to a nearby stream and gather fresh water to bring back to the camp. Simon found a large boulder that would hide the flames from the fire from view of any potential spies. He also made sure to quickly get the flame very hot; to reduce the smoke so they couldn't be tracked. All the men worked together to help one another. They could feel the end of the war and could smell home in the air. This put them in a good mood and masked the horror of battle and their lost forever comrades.

Even though Curtis and Amnon had set up a perimeter watch; none of Calder's men went looking for them. The food was good and kept the men happy. They joked and told stories often to pass the time. Aaron would sometimes take one of the walking sentry's watches. This was his gesture to show his men he was still right there with them. Aaron's men did appreciate this even though they never said it aloud. Aaron didn't need them to say it out loud, he could tell by their faces and the men's morale. He was bold and strong but also very companionate towards his men. He would often tell his men that no one could mess with them and get away with it, except him.

Three days later John and his men attacked Calder in what they believed to be their final battle before overall victory. However, Calder and his men were barricaded inside. Only archers sending random volleys would play apart in this battle. It began to rain and the sound of pinging rain drops filled the air as they bounced off of the men's armor. Aaron looked at John and said "I don't think they like the rain" John didn't seem amused by Aaron at the moment. John grew impatient and suggested to Curtis "We should cut down a tree and break down the gate" Curtis agreed and called back the men. It would take two days to get a tree the size they needed and trim it where it could be used. John and his men went back to their camp and began to look for the perfect tree.

When the rain finally lifted some men went out in search of the tree that would act as a battering ram. The other men stoked their fires and dried their clothes. Laughter broke out as the men told each other stories of childhood and their dealings with different women. The morale stayed high and the nervousness of war and battle slowly diminished. To many of the men this felt like the old days when they would camp out in the woods with their friends. Most of the men longed for home but for this brief instance they were happy and content.

Finally the tree that would be used to break down the gate at the Castle of Aodhan had been found. Many of the men took turns with their axes and slowly took the bottom of this massive oak away piece by piece. When it fell the entire camp jumped from being startled. It was very loud as it crashed through smaller trees on its way to the ground. When it hit the ground even a few archers from atop the wall of Calder's high jacked castle could hear the echo coming from the woods. Aaron had his foot soldiers begin hacking away at the huge branches and the bark. Simon readied his men to soon pull the tree from where it laid using ropes and their horses. This was a joint effort and John was pleased with the work the men had put in. He thought perhaps the men felt the faster they completed this, the faster they would claim victory and return home. Because this is how he felt and he too took up an axe and began to help.

CHAPTER IX

BERSERKERS

While John and his men looked to break into the castle; Calder meant to reinforce it. He sent out men to also gather trees and make a wall in front of the gate. He would build as many obstacles to keep John out for as long as he could. His men began sharpening large branches and sticking them in the ground in hopes of stopping Simons riders. Calder only needed to slow John and his men from entering because a small fifteen hundred man Berserker army would soon be on the way.

Berserkers were ferocious warriors that were merciless. They used their axes to destroy a man rather than kill him. Some of their swords and axes were longer than the men themselves and Berserkers stood between six and a half to seven feet tall. The Berserkers believed that the only way to be a leader was to prove one's self in battle. Once proven that they were a fierce warrior they would be allowed to challenge the current leader. Three things could happen in this event. One: the one challenging would be killed by the current leader. Two: the current leader could willingly hand over the title. Three: the current leader would be slain and the new leader would take his place.

In the event that a Berserker leader died of other causes his heir would take the title until challenged. If there is no heir then the next in command of the leader takes over until challenged. They had no laws, if one felt that he had been wronged; then it was up to him to kill the one who wronged him and make it right. The Berserkers didn't take wives they simply grabbed which ever woman was alone and claimed her for the time being. When the man had finished spending time with her; he would send her back out to be claimed by the next man in search of a woman.

The Berserkers live in the Black Wood because it is easy to conceal themselves and wild animals are plentiful. The woods there are dark and burn bright. Since Berserkers don't have wives they share their women; they usually lose track of who is kin and who isn't. Therefore, they call each other brother. In older times before Kingdoms had been set up and lands claimed. Berserkers fought off any threat that landed on the shores of Adalrikr. When there was no threat they would trade meat for weapons. The Berserkers became known to other Kingdoms as wild mad men who only loved to kill and mutilate the bodies of their victims. Killing became more of a sport then a necessity to the Berserkers.

Grog had already made it to Adalrikr as Calder continued to reinforce the Castle of Aodhan. John and his men had no idea what was unfolding while they quickly cut the branches from the large oak tree. It took three days to get the tree ready and another three to get it to the front of the castle. Horses pulled the huge oak down the hill as fifteen men on either side guided it. There was still mud on the ground which made it difficult to move. Some of the horses would get stuck and have to be pulled out. Handles were notched in the wood from front to back on both sides. There were enough handles for twenty men on each side of this gigantic tree.

John attacked the Castle of Aodhan every day for a week. His men would pick up the tree in the morning and try to pound through the heavy gate that was also made of oak. At the end of each night John's men would carry the tree back about twenty yards and leave it there for the next day. Every night Calder would have his last two to three hundred men go out and set up the obstacles that took John and his men nearly three hours a day to get around. Curtis and his archers kept the men covered as they used the tree to beat against the gate. From time to time Calder's men would shoot arrows at them from above the castle wall. The enemy archers could never get a clean shot off due to Curtis and Amnon's continuous watch. Every time an enemy archer would appear Curtis or Amnon gave the order to fire.

It seemed as if this would be a never ending war. Simon and his riders waited patiently as the men beat on the gate seeking entrance. Simon wanted the gate to fly open and a legion of the enemy to pile out; but he was unlucky in his silent request. John and Aaron would stand with their men and wait for any signal that the castle gate had been breached. Aaron was restless and bored. He started making up games as he would walk through the ranks of his men. Every few rows a couple soldiers would lose their composure and burst out laughing. John would give a cold look down the line just in time to see Aaron stroll away from the men.

In John's mind this was good for the men to laugh and Aaron being so short yet fierce was just the right man for the job. Sometimes his jokes were so vulgar, instead of hearing laughter at the punch line; the men would give a sound of disgust. When this would happen Aaron would put his hands behind his back and continue walking down the line with a smile on his face.

It wasn't until the eighth day John's men split the massive gate down the middle. The oak tree had finally beaten the large oak gate. It was getting late in the day and many men had taken their turn with hurling the large tree into the gate. John called to his men to return to their camp. The men were tired and John said to his Captains "Tomorrow we break down the gate and end this war". Even Curtis looked hopeful at the idea. None of the men had expected such a large force to be on Aodhan. Many of them believed that this wouldn't be an all out war but a mere few battles. Their blood stained clothes told a different story.

Many of the men were pierced by an arrow, a sword, or an axe. As their wounds healed slowly they would dream of their families. John was one of these men that often dreamed of home. The night sky gleamed over the men as they slept. Some of the men looked up at it. They noticed the dark spots in the sky that seemed to lead for an eternity; next to these spots was a bright star light that lit up the sky. The moon too was very bright that night and seemed very close. What appeared to be mountains could be seen on the surface of this dazzling planet like structure.

Meanwhile Grog had reached his leader and told him of Calder's acceptance. The Berserker leader looked to his men and told them to prepare for war. He called for his son

"Denrel!" A man in his mid twenties with long scraggly black hair and a short thin beard, no more than six inches appeared out of his bony chin. "Yes father" he said. "You will lead these men. Once you have complete control of Aodhan I will join you with the rest of our men" the leader said in a low confident voice. Denrel turned and left without a word. This would be his first battle but not his first time killing. He had earned the title of warrior at the young age of thirteen; when a full grown Berserker tried taking his fresh deer kill. Denrel pulled his blade and challenged him. Even though Denrel was the leader's son, he challenged another Berserker and that could not be reversed. He was victorious in his duel against the other man and fought proudly before his father's eyes. This earned him his title and now he wanted to live up to it. Denrel and his men gathered their weapons and marched to the north shore of Adalrikr.

King Arvid received his message from the man that carried the head of Arvid's messenger. He was furious and in a rage. He called to his Captain "Prepare my army! We ride for Aodhan in the morning!" the man tried to tell the King of the Berserkers but King Arvid stormed to his chambers to dig out his battle armor and the man was thrown out of the castle by a large soldier.

The next morning the Berserker army met Arvid's army face to face at the north shore. Arvid met with Denrel alone and away from their armies. Both sides were ready to attack one another. Two thousand of Arvid's men against fifteen hundred wild blood thirsty Berserkers. After ten minutes of talking Arvid returned to his men and told them to follow him back to his castle. Denrel had told Arvid of the alliance between his father and Calder. Arvid not wanting another war against the Berserkers agreed to call off his hunt for Calder; if the Berserkers agreed to help Arvid if he were to receive blame for Calder's actions by the other Kingdoms and be attacked. Denrel agreed to the Kings request only to not prolong any more time. The Berserkers began to board Calder's ships he had sent to Adalrikr for them. Arvid had his ships brought back up on shore before he and his army returned to their castle. Arvid was furious but was no fool either; he knew an attack on the Berserker leader's son would surely have the consequence of death.

The next day in Aodhan John finally took down the gate. His men had been at it all day and the sun had turned many of the men's skin red. Calder's men didn't put up any kind of fight when the gate slowly fell to either side. The wood had been blackened by the attempts to burn it. The men from inside the castle could hear the gate crack and splinter. When it finally gave the massive boom sounded like a dozen swords clashing together all at once. One of John's men mentioned the sound being like the thunder when they had crossed the dangerous Sea of Arrachtaigh. There was finally nothing stopping the men of Carraig from ending this evil tyrant.

However, John's men were so tired from the task of bringing the gate fully down to the ground this time; he didn't want to risk a large number of casualties. He called his men back and they retired to their camp. Han and Edmond had been given the task of hunting and trapping. Every night they returned with enough food to feed John's entire army. While eating Han came up to John and said "While I was out today I ran across an old friend. He told me that Adeen has an army now and is ready to march down from

Alexander" John looked up and asked "How many men?" Han replied "Almost a thousand". John turned to Simon and said "Send a rider to Adeen and tell him we are days away from victory and I will send for him when we have won this war" Simon got up and went to find a messenger. John did not want Adeen to bring his men and try to claim some of the victory. This was John's first war and he wanted his name in the tongues of those telling the story. He was not a conceded man but he wanted his men that had given their lives; to be forever remembered as the men of Carraig who conquered the enemy pillagers. Not the men who helped the soldiers of Aodhan conquer them. It was a simple request but this request also could prevent a quicker victory.

The next morning he gathered his men and began to tell them "You have all fought bravely and there are no other men I would ever want to stand beside in battle. My father is looking down on us with a smile. We have earned this victory! So let's end this and get back home to Carraig! Where we belong!" the men shouted with good morale. "Simon, lead the charge" John said with confidence. Simon took off with the rest of his riders and blew the trumpet of the North. All of Simon's riders carried a grin on their faces. This had been a long awaited goal of theirs. Day after day the riders would sit at the edge of the castle wall waiting for the men to put a hole in the gate large enough to fit riders through. That day had finally come and Simon could be seen from the enemy lookout leading his riders down the hillside.

Calder knew this was the last time he could hold off the men of Carraig. He called all of his men to the broken gate and said "Fight with everything you have! We will not retreat or try to make for the ships. After you kill ten of them I give you permission to die!" Calder's men had been living off of the food stock piled in the castle. They were well rested in luxurious beds and ready to fight.

Simon and his riders maneuvered around the obstacles. They broke down the make shift gate that Calder's men had constructed and stormed in the castle to begin the fight. Curtis as usual left the archers to Amnon and joined John and Aaron with the foot soldiers. The gate's opening was large but with all of the debris only five men could pass through at a time. All of the Captains and John entered the castle. This was a brutal fight; Calder's men were cutting down the men of Carraig. Calder himself fought with a fierce sense of survival. John's men greatly outnumbered Calder's men but only a few soldiers at a time could gain access inside the castle. Calder's men were ready for them as they passed through the demolished gate. Eventually a decent amount of John's men had made it through.

Curtis turned to his left and saw Calder strike down one of his old friends. Curtis picked up a sword now having one in each hand and ran towards Calder. The two locked eyes and Calder had a smile on his face; he had seen Curtis in action and dreamed of the day he would be able to face him. The two struck swords so hard they both broke in half and shot sparks flying in the air. Curtis immediately put his other sword in his right hand and Calder pulled another sword from his waist. They fought each other violently and men from both sides stopped to watch. The mighty Captain from Carraig showed every man there how powerful he truly was. Calder moved from side to side dodging would be fatal blows from Curtis. John rounded the corner just in time to see Calder move out of the way of Curtis's blade and come back severing Curtis's arm from the elbow. Curtis let out a horrid scream and John's jaw dropped. Aaron heard Curtis and began to run in his direction. The men stopped watching and began to fight one another again. John started to fight his way to Curtis. Curtis had fallen to one knee and his blood poured out of his arm. He looked at the ground where his arm lay still clutching his sword. Calder stood in front of Curtis looking at him in hopes that he would pick up the sword so he could finish him off worthily.

Aaron made his way towards Calder fighting one man at a time. John also came within ear shot of Curtis. John yelled "I'm coming Curtis" and Curtis whispered back "He's mine" Curtis reached for his sword with his left hand and rose to his feet. Calder came at him with everything he had. Curtis backed up while holding his blade up in defense; Calder came down over and over again cracking down on him with superior power. With one last burst of energy Curtis moved towards him and began swinging wildly with a glow in his eyes and a smile on his face.

Aaron reached Curtis and began to fight Calder with him. Aaron took most of Calder's attention from Curtis but it wasn't enough. Aaron slipped on Curtis's blood and went down to one knee. Calder saw this and lunged at the opportunity; striking down hard at Aaron's head but Curtis turned his back to Calder and blocked his fatal blow. It was a suicide move because he was using his left hand and would not be able to turn back around fast enough to counter the next swing. Curtis knew this and did it anyway to save Aaron's life. Aaron rose back to his feet just as Calder thrust his sword into Curtis's back and into his heart. Curtis fell to his knees and the light left his eyes a few seconds later. Aaron stood in shock for a few seconds and then faced Calder. John finally had fought his way to Aaron and Curtis; he looked down at his friend and realized he was too late.

John looked back at Calder with eyes that could kill. He said to Aaron "Take the men and finish everyone here" Aaron didn't move, he was fixed on avenging his friend and all of his countrymen that had died because of this man called Calder. John said it again and Aaron finally turned in a rage and left Calder to John. John never lost his eye contact as Calder moved closer. "Now you die" John said softly as he gripped his sword with both hands. Calder swung first and their blades cracked like lightning. Back and forth they swung at each other. Calder would jump over fallen soldiers and John would follow. The two fought each other without paying any attention to the other soldiers around them. They continued this until John sliced Calder across the chest. Calder backed up and gasped for air but John showed no mercy he attacked again and sliced him once more this time across the front of his leg. Calder walked backwards with a limp sensing his end. Just then Simon rode up to John yelling "John, there is an army running this way from the south! We have to pull out of the castle!" John looked at Simon and saw the intensity on his face. "Pull everyone out and form the line" John told Simon while not being fully conscious of what he had just been told.

John wouldn't be able to finish this duel with Calder now and he knew it. "I'll be seeing you again real soon" he said to Calder as he ran out of the castle. Calder only had twenty men left and they were all injured to some degree. John mounted a horse and went to the front of the line. He looked to the south and saw the fifteen hundred Berserker warriors running full speed at his army. "Amnon, you are my new Captain of the archers" John proclaimed. "Yes sire" Amnon replied. Amnon knew that could only mean one thing; his Captain and mentor had fallen and were now dead. He led the archers to the front and when the Berserkers were in range he unleashed a never ending rain cloud of arrows at them.

The Berserkers had spread out and were at different depths of one another making it hard to pin point a target for the archers. John called off the archers and sent in Simon and his riders. John quickly found out that his mere twelve hundred were no match for the Berserkers. They ripped through John's men like cloth. Their weapons were so long that by the time John's men could reach them they had already been cut in two.

The Berserkers kept fighting and John's numbers quickly dropped to below a thousand men and only ten Berserkers had been slain. John yelled for the retreat and his men ran for their camp. Simon and Amnon worked together to keep the Berserkers off the retreating foot soldiers. Simon had blood running down his face due to his head being split open from one side to the other. He wrapped it up and went to find his King. Soon after the foot soldiers made it up the hillside; Simon and Amnon's men quickly followed. John and his bloody comrades had made it to a temporary safety which they were familiar with. At this point all the men of Carraig knew that this war had just doubled its magnitude. They looked at one another in despair. Their hopes and longing for a victory had just faded. In their hearts they knew if their king did not call a full retreat; their souls would be lost to wonder the land of Aodhan. The once strong and powerful morale that kept the men sharp and together was now lost on their previous battle field.

As John watched from above the Berserkers brought many weapons into the castle and they set up their camp. Simon looked at John and said "They are going to come for us and we can't attack them. They are warriors and they are fresh. We have been fighting for over a month and they have only been fighting for an hour" John nodded his head at Simon and said "Have the men pack up camp. We march for Alexander tonight, Han and Edmond will lead the way".

CHAPTER X

CALDER'S FINAL STAND

As John's men packed up their camp and cleaned their wounds; Amnon and two of his archers walked into camp with one of Calder's men. His hands were bound behind his back, with string from a bow. Amnon walked in front while his archers held each of the prisoner's arms. "King John, my men found this scout only a hundred yards away" Amnon said. John looked at the prisoner and saw blood running down his arms. "Who are these new warriors? They are not like Calder and the others" John asked. The prisoner looked down and refused to answer. "You will answer or I'll throw you off this cliff" Amnon said in all seriousness. John watched as the prisoner smiled, he was bleeding from his mouth as well. His long golden hair turned red as the breeze blew it in his face. "If you tell me what I wish to know, you shall live and return to your master" John told the prisoner. "How can I trust you?" the prisoner said with a smirk. "I give you my word as the

King of Carraig. If that is not good enough for you; you can take your chances with my Captain" John said annoyed.

The prisoner looked at Amnon and then back to John "These men are the Berserkers of the Black Woods from Adalrikr. Wild men... Mad men... Whose only desire is to kill. They heard of Calder and offered to give us aide. Calder is wounded and his men are all but destroyed". John looked at Aaron with eyes of despair. The prisoner continued telling the history of the Berserkers. He told them this out of vengeance not fear. He liked seeing the faces on the men as he explained the nature of the Berserkers. "Take him to the bottom of the hill and release him" John told Amnon. Amnon motioned to his archers and they headed out of the camp. Aaron reminded John of Adeen and his thousand Aodhan warriors that waited in Alexander. John agreed with Aaron and they prepared all the men to march north to the Castle of Alexander. When the men heard of the army waiting to aide them at Alexander; a spark of hope entered their hearts once more. Perhaps this hope was just enough to make it north to the castle. Perhaps it was enough for one last fight as well. Amnon escorted the prisoner down the wooded trail that Simon had made in the previous weeks with his riders. Amnon would say things to the prisoner in hopes of him leading the Berserkers in the wrong direction. He made false comments to his men about the far east and the men they had waiting there.

It was too late though, he had already overheard John say he was retreating to the Castle of Alexander. The prisoner had also heard him speak of more soldiers waiting there. Amnon continued to walk him down the path. The sun began to set and little glimpses of light would peek through the trees as they made their way down the hill. Amnon tried to strike up a conversation with his prisoner in hopes of gaining more information. "So, Calder is a lord in Adalrikr? Or is he just a rouge warrior?" Amnon said in a sarcastic tone. The prisoner kept his eyes on the ground and didn't respond. "You know, it's a good thing you talked and gave up your master. It looked as if that cliff would have been a painful fall" Amnon continued in hopes of angering his captive. The prisoner looked up at Amnon and gave a small chuckle as he said "You know nothing about the men that hunt you now. In a few days all that you know will be destroyed"

One of Amnon's men gave him a quick elbow to the ribs. The prisoner gasped for air as Amnon laughed and said "We will see about that. I personally predict an arrow ending your days and as for the Berserkers; it will be a nice change in battling an opponent worth killing. No more farmers in warriors clothing such as you and your men" they reached the bottom and could see the castle. Amnon cut the bindings that held the prisoner and released him. The prisoner stumbled in the dark towards the Castle of Aodhan; as Amnon and his men ran back up the hillside towards their camp.

Back in Carraig Michael kept the borders patrolled with many men. He took the task of patrolling the North Capital as well. James made sure the West was secure all the way to Michael's border as well as all the way south to Daniel's. Michael began to grow impatient; there had not been any news of his brother John in some time. He sent a messenger to the Port of the North to find out what he could. Michael didn't want to risk the lives of any of his soldiers by sending them across the treacherous Sea of Arrachtaigh. Instead he called several villages around the east to the East Capital. When the villagers arrived they stood together at the gate of Michael's castle. "I will pay every man his weight in gold if you travel to Aodhan and bring me word of my brother King John!" Michael shouted from the wall of his castle while looking down at the men. The crowd began to whisper back and forth to one another. After five minutes went by one man stepped forward and hollered up to his King "I will go! But I want half now to go to my family and the other half when I return". Michael immediately replied "Done! Who will accompany this man?" Slowly four men emerged from the crowd each of them looked hesitant but they agreed to join if the same terms Michael gave the first man applied.

Michael paid the men's families and gave each of them a horse to ride for the North Harbor. When the men arrived an old fisherman came up to them. "Do you need a guide? Looks like you might be traveling to Aodhan. I was there around two months ago" the old fisherman exclaimed. The men looked at each other and one of them said "How much?" Quickly the old fisherman replied "How much are your lives worth? Perhaps ten silver coins each?" The men looked outraged with the price but a wrong move on this Sea could very well mean their lives so they agreed and paid him. The six men climbed aboard one of the ships that had been left behind and began to row while the old man steered.

Half way through their journey they asked the old fisherman "How much longer?" he replied in a critical voice "King John was much in a rush to get to Aodhan as well. But soon you will find out like he did that the journey of getting there is the hard part" the men looked at him with concern and one of them asked "What do you mean by that? These waters are calm enough" the old man grinned and said "Look up ahead at that storm coming our way" the men looked but couldn't see anything. The fisherman smiled and said "When the weather gets bad and the monsters of the deep come up to the surface to play. Just remember one thing...Row" one of the men got up and went to the other side of the boat and scoffed "He's just messing with us" the other men kept their comments to themselves and starred at the direction the old man had warned them about. They looked uneasy because these men had heard the stories of the treacherous Sea of Arrachtaigh.

James and Daniel were having their own concerns and Daniel rode with his personal guard to the West Capital to speak with his brother. When he arrived James was overjoyed to see him. Both of them asked simultaneously if the other had heard any news of John. Both quietly replied "no". James told his wife Rahkel to have the kitchens prepare a feast for his brother. Then the two sat side by side while a servant poured them ale. They talked a great deal about their father and of John. Niether one admitted to the other that they were feeling remorse for not joining John. They drunk the night away and for the most part seemed happy. This was mostly because neither one of them slept good since John left and being together made them feel closer to him in a way. They discussed how John must be leading his army to glory on the battle field and how he must be slaying his enemy just like their father had done. Little did they know their brother John and his men were about to be running for their lives through the Plains of Gronn in the Kingdom of Aodhan.

The Berserkers had seen Amnon's prisoner get released. They questioned him and he told them what had happened; he also told them John's men were packing up camp in a hurry. Denrel yelled for his Berserkers "Get ready to march!" Denrel told the former prisoner to lead the way to the camp. One of John's lookouts came to him quickly and reported "The Berserkers are on the move. They are heading right for us!" John rose to his feet and yelled to his Captains "Get your men out of here now! Han! You take Simon and his men. Aaron you're with me and Edmond will guide us. Amnon, give us some time. Hold them off as long as you can and follow our tracks to Alexander!" Every man in John's army moved as fast as they could. Simon's riders were the first to leave in only a matter of minutes. Then John, Aaron, and the rest of the foot soldiers followed Edmond through the trees.

Amnon moved his men to the top of the hill and waited for the Berserkers to arrive. He spread out his men in all directions. Amnon yelled to his men "We need to give the King a good head start! No one moves until I say!" Amnon was not Curtis but he still had the respect of his men. Every archer stood his ground and waited for the enemy to approach. The Berserkers could be heard marching up the path towards Amnon and his men. Suddenly a dark tall figure came in to Amnon's view. Amnon drew back his bow and waited; when over ten Berserkers could be seen clearly he released. The Berserker fell on his face and the rest of Amnon's archers fired. Four more Berserkers fell, before the rest scattered into the trees. The Berserkers were used to traveling in thick woods and they moved with speed Amnon had never seen. The archers held off the Berserkers for a little over thirty minutes; killing only twelve. But it gave John and his men the time they needed to escape with their lives. Amnon told his men to fall back and they hurried through the woods. Amnon and his men knew this path very well now and made double the time over the Berserkers. They made it back to the empty camp were the fires had been doused. Amnon ordered loudly "Don't stop, keep moving!" The archers ran past the camp and followed the trail that Simon's horses had recently made. "If they continue to follow us, we will need to set up again and slow them down!" Amnon shouted out for all of his archers to hear. He knew that it would be up to him to make sure the rest of the soldiers reached Alexander. Amnon was ready for this and with his new title of Captain, welcomed it. In his heart, he felt Curtis's mighty loyalty and courage. This pushed him harder, he would not let down his old Captain and friend.

It was dark and John could barely see in front of him. Edmond led the way and with every quick movement John would call out his name "Edmond!?" Edmond would respond quickly "Over here! Keep moving" John's men moved as fast as they could, following one another through the forest. From time to time Aaron could be heard over the confusion saying "Of all the nights, this is the only one in a month where the moon doesn't decide to shine so bright it keeps everyone awake" small sounds of laughter could be heard from the men surrounding him. John would then holler back at them "Well we know we didn't lose Aaron back there. I was concerned when we passed over that log that he might not make it over" again the men laughed. Aaron was quick to rebuttal "Hey! I remember when you had to use a mounting block to get on your horse" "I was nine years old Aaron and we were the same height. The only difference is I kept growing" the men chuckled out loud at the friendly duel their King and Captain had engaged in. It wasn't until Edmond yelled back at them that they all became silent "Well, if your goal is to lead the enemy straight to us; you're doing a good job" they continued through the dark woods in search of the clearing that marked the border between the Woods of Stillhet and the Plains of Gronn.

Once the Berserkers made it to the top they sifted through the abandoned camp. They took what they wanted; a few swords and some fresh food and water. Denrel was not prepared for a full on foot pursuit so he called his Berserkers back down to the Castle of Aodhan were they would gather their things and prepare to hunt down King John and the last of his men.

The sun had come up and the men were exhausted. They passed a stream where the men could take a quick drink. Aaron was so covered in dirt and sweat that he jumped into the stream head first. "Good job Aaron, now try and run while you just added twenty pounds to your clothing" John said in a cocky voice. "It's better to run cool than run hot and pass out. Plus the sun is out and will dry me off in no time" Aaron said in a defensive voice.

Simon and his riders were two hundred yards in front of John in case there would be a need to turn around. John continued a fast pace even though some of his soldiers were wounded. Aaron suddenly yelled out "Riders approaching!" John looked up to see three riders carrying a flag from

Aodhan. Simon went out to meet them. "Are you the men of Carraig?" one man asked. Simon replied "Yes, where is your army?" the man looked at the other two before replying "Alexander of course. We have come to receive word from King John" Simon pointed at the fleeing troops and said "King John is there. We need to get to Alexander quickly; a new army is approaching called the Berserkers and we will need every man left in Aodhan to defeat them" the riders looked concerned as they turned around and one of them said "Follow us". They would act as the new guides to the castle.

After a full night and then day's journey John gave the order to camp. Simon and his men joined the foot soldiers and they split up the night watch. After a few hours one of Simon's men rode up to him and said "Amnon and his men are approaching from the south" Simon went to John and told him of the news. Once Amnon reached the camp he was greeted by John. Amnon told John what had happened. "They never passed the clearing. My guess is they went back to the castle to retrieve their things. They will most likely be on our trail at first light if they have not left already" Amnon told John in his deep voice. "We will march all day tomorrow. The sooner we are behind the walls of our own castle the better. Hopefully Adeen's men are not as old as he is" John said with a forced smile. Everyone around were too exhausted to return the smile back.

John looked up at the sky and wondered if his father would still be proud. He thought about Elaine and could hear her voice in his head "Just come home now". For a second he pondered if maybe he should go home. He lost so many men and would be held accountable for that in the eyes of his people. Then he remembered something his father had once told him "I lost many men in my life but I always came out victorious and that made it worth it to them and their families" when John remembered these words he felt a spark of energy pulse through his body. He knew at that moment he would not leave Aodhan until he was either victorious or dead. The men that fell fighting for what he believed in would not be dishonored by their king retreating home. He closed his eyes and dreamed of his battle strategy for when he reached the Castle of Alexander.

Simon had one of his men sew up his head. Aaron received a three inch gash from Calder; he too had him sew up his wound. Many of the men were so tired they didn't bother rinsing off their blood stained bodies. That could all be done once they reached the safe haven of Alexander. With the exception of the men on watch the entire army slept all through the night. They had reached the edge of the Plains of Gronn and the beginning of the Woods of Dyr. It would not be too long before they were where they started; at the shores of Aodhan next to the Castle of Alexander. Some of the men felt a little closer to home knowing their ships were not too far away.

The men dreamed of holding their loved ones in their arms. Except for a few that dreamed of losing their loved ones in battle. One boy had lost his father in the first battle and he would wake up in the night crying out. None of the men criticized him for this; a few that were sleeping close by would simply say "It's just a dream. You're safe, go back to sleep" all of the men had suffered this sort of loss in one way or another. Some had lost a father or son; others had lost a brother or uncle and all of them had lost a friend. They dealt with this sorrow in their own ways. Many would focus on home and the loved ones that awaited their return. This is how John dealt with his pain from the loss of his men.

The next morning the Berserker army made its way through Aodhan. Although, Calder was out in front he no longer led his own campaign. Calder was now more of a guide even though he had only heard the direction of Aodhan through his scouts. Calder's men were badly injured and half of them could not make the trip to Alexander. The Berserkers were growing tired of the slow and useless men holding them back. Denrel went to Calder and told him "When we get to this King John you will lead the attack with your men. My men will be right behind you" Calder looked at him and replied "Why don't you lead the attack and we will follow?" Denrel chuckled and said "No, this is your campaign. You are the mighty Calder and you will lead" Denrel looked behind him at his next in command and laughed while saying "Isn't that right Grog?" Grog smiled back at him and said "That's right". Calder knew their plan and he began to make his own. In his head he planned to lead the battle but after the fighting began he would sneak out and return to his few men left behind in the Castle of Aodhan. Then he and his men would make their way to a ship and sail for Adalrikr. Calder didn't want any more part of this alliance with these Berserkers. His men were all but destroyed and he too was badly injured. Calder had seen enough bloodshed himself and was now ready to go home and regroup. In his mind he planned to regain more men and eventually raid again but this time more west to the Kingdom of Hag which joined with Dolg on the same island. He had taken Dolg and expected Hag would be no different. This would be the last time he attempted to raid a kingdom so close to Carraig.

John's men got up with the sun and his army was making good time, the men could feel home and this gave them energy. They knew that with Adeen's army they could defeat the Berserkers and go home. Simon seemed to be feeling better as did Aaron. Amnon stayed back with his archers as Curtis often did. The army was a lot less in number from last time it crossed these paths. They were injured but with the less numbers they traveled in half the time. With every village and house they passed John would warn them of what was coming. Many of the people left and the others went underground into shelters they had built. When John crossed the farm of the thirteen year old boy he was nowhere to be seen. John went to the door to warn him but all that remained was a message carved on the door that read "Father, I am going to Alexander to join the Kings army. If you are reading this I will be home after the war" John returned to his men and they continued north.

John pushed his men to keep marching in the night; they could see the lanterns of Alexander from where they were. "We're almost there. Keep going not much further" Simon hollered to the men. Their pace quickened and their hearts felt heavy. It had been months since the men had slept in a castle rather than the woods. Adeen's three riders announced their presence and the enormous gate began to lower. This gate was different from the swinging doors that the men had broken into at the Castle of Aodhan. This gate was much older, still made of oak but dropped down from chains rather that closed and sealed with a giant log. John and Aaron were first to enter. Adeen slowly walked towards them as if his age had doubled in the past few months. "Tell me everything John" Adeen said in an old slow voice. John and his Captains met with Adeen and a few of his men. Over a few hours John with the help of Simon, Aaron, and Amnon told them of everything that had happened from their last meeting. They told him of the first camp they had destroyed. Then they continued with the attack and retreat of the first battle at the castle. Amnon took the story over at the end with the Berserkers chasing him and his men up the hillside. Adeen looked concerned and his eyes glared at the ground in hatred. He looked at John and said "My men and yours together will put an end to these tyrants. Together our men will avenge every lost soul and family" With that being said Adeen got up and headed for his chamber.

John's men settled in and were given rooms; these rooms were not much but they were ten times better than sleeping in the dirt. Hot food and cold drinks were laid before them and for the first time in Aodhan the men felt joy. "Live it up now because in the next few days we are right back at it" Amnon said in an upbringing voice. The injured were given medicine and their wounds were cared for. Black smiths repaired weapons and armor including Roman and Cain's who by this point needed almost full restoration. Cain had a broken rib and hadn't seen a fight in many weeks. Roman rarely left John's side during combat. Both dogs needed mending but for the most part they were sound.

All of the men received new clothes and were cleaned off by the bathing pool inside the castle. When the men finally lay down to sleep they felt nearly back to normal. This lasted for three days until one afternoon a scout rode in and reported a large war party heading towards Alexander.

The men knew the time had come and prepared for battle. Night fell and the fires of the Berserkers could be seen from the castle walls. It seemed the Berserkers were weary from the long march and decided to make camp. "One more day I guess" John said to Adeen. Adeen replied with "One more day for these heathens to live" John smiled at Adeen's confidence but knew what these men were capable of. It was going to be a long bloody battle with many lives lost but John was ready and so were his men. John gathered his Captains and told them to visit with the men. He went to the foot soldiers first and sat with a few of them. John talked with them and gave them words of encouragement. Amnon did the same with the archers and Simon went to his riders. Aaron went to the other side of the foot soldiers and inspired a few laughs. John found Harold and sat with him the longest. Harold told John of his family back home including the girl that had his interest. John said to him "I will give everything I have left to make sure you return home. Someday you may very well be a Captain" with a half hearted smile Harold nodded in acceptance.

Simon found Aral sitting with Marcus and began a conversation. Simon told Aral he would be forever remembered for his gallant bravery during this war. He continued by saying the same to Marcus but was interrupted by Aaron "Hey, quit trying to recruit my foot soldiers to be riders" The three looked at Aaron; Simon and Aral then looked at Marcus. Aaron too looked at Marcus and said "Well, maybe that's not what you're doing" Marcus with a forced fake smile looked back at Aaron and said "No Captain, they aren't trying to give me a horse" Aaron smiled and said "Just making sure" and with that Aaron continued his walk.

The next morning all of John and Adeen's men were in full battle formation outside of the castle walls. Amnon led the archers from atop the castle wall. Simon and his riders stayed hidden to the left flank. John set tall on his horse and was ready for battle. Within moments Amnon gave the signal to his archers to open fire. Nine men were out in front and around fourteen hundred well armed Berserkers followed behind. Calder led with his last eight men and when John saw him he sounded the charge. Around eighteen hundred men ran straight for the Berserker army. Arrows continued to fly over John's army and into Berserker bodies. John met Calder head to head and their rematch began. Calder's other eight men were swallowed up by John's foot soldiers except for one who tried running away from the battle. He ran right into Grog who showed him no mercy and relieved him of his life.

The Berserkers axes could be heard all around the battle field. They had a high pitch whistle when swung through the air and made a loud clash when struck with metal. The Berserkers would yell at the top of their lungs when they made a kill. This was almost a badge of honor; a code between warlords about the count of their kills. Hundreds of men fell in the first hour of battle including Calder. John jumped from his horse and split Calder's head in half along with most of his body. Curtis had been avenged and Aaron's guilt went away after witnessing John's maniacal move. Calder had been suffering from his already inflicted wounds. After being forced to travel through Aodhan at the speed of the Berserkers he had no energy. He could barley raise his sword to defend himself. When John jumped down from his horse he had the look of dominant vengeance in his eyes. There would be no backup plan in Calder's future. His body now lay before the Castle of Alexander and would remain there to rot.

Thirty yards away from him Grog swung his axe in a circle and decapitated four men at once. Amnon saw this and put three arrows in his left shoulder but it had no effect. Grog continued cutting down John's men one by one until he came face to face with Aaron. Grog towered Aaron and Aaron liked it that way. Aaron moved in and out of Grog's reach he was too fast for the huge Berserker. Grog pulled back his axe and swung it over his shoulder at Aaron. Aaron moved to the side of the huge axe as it hit the ground. Aaron put one foot on the axe to hold it to the ground; he leapt off of it and into the air while slicing Grogs head in half from his left eye to the right side of his chin.

Simon drove his riders through the left side of the Berserker army. They fought hard and Aral took down many Berserkers as he passed them. After five minutes of this the Berserker army turned its focus to Simon and the riders. Suddenly Aral's horse had been injured and could no longer run. Aral jumped off of him and swatted him back towards the castle. Three Berserkers saw this and headed for him while holding their axes high. Aral was ready for them and as the first one made his swing; Aral gracefully moved and returned the blow with a fatal strike of his sword to the back of his enemy's neck. When the next Berserker made his attempt towards Aral; Simon rode passed and killed him from behind with one swing of his sword. The third

Berserker came quickly at Simon and knocked him off his horse with a strong blow.

Simon got to his feet and together with Aral attacked him. He fought the two of them with great strength. Aral took out one of his legs with an upward motion of his sword and Simon came down hard with his and ended the fight. Simon retrieved his horse and Aral climbed on the back. Simon rode hard towards Aaron's men to drop off Aral with his brother Marcus.

When the two reached Aaron and his men; Aral jumped off and found his brother. They began to fight side by side as Simon returned to his riders. Marcus yelled to his brother "What happened to your horse?" and Aral replied "He's a little lame at the moment, so I figured I'd join you in beating these bastards. Then we can go home" Marcus looked over to him and said "Sounds good to me. Just stay close to me and listen for Aaron's orders to move" the two continued to fight together. Every now and again Aral would require a little assistance but Marcus was always close enough to provide it. The battle raged for hours and the brutality was never ending. There were more men slain on this day than any other battle in Carraig history. As the death toll rose, John knew that his wounded warriors could not keep up for much longer. He too was battle weary and in much need of rest.

Denrel didn't expect John's men to fight so gallantly and fiercely. He called his men off the attack after hearing that Grog, his next in command, had been slain by the hands of Aaron. John yelled for his men to return back to the castle once he saw the Berserkers in full retreat. After the men returned to the castle John called for a death count on both sides. Simon came to report an hour later "Six hundred of ours dead and three hundred of theirs" John looked uneasy at Simon and said "Those numbers will not pull off a victory. Tomorrow we will stay behind the castle walls and see how we do". Most of the men slain were Adeen's; the farmers from this land could not match up to the skilled fighting force of the Berserker army.

Denrel cursed his men for not finishing off John and his army. He was furious and let his men know. Back in the Black Wood of Adalrikr, Denrel's father gathered five hundred of his fiercest men and headed towards Aodhan to see for himself the progress his son had made with Calder. He did not know that Calder and all of his men were slain by John and his army; nor did he know his son had taken up the campaign himself. He was in full march to witness the success of his army. Denrel's father brought with him these men as a personal guard; not intending to use them in assisting his son. In his eyes this was a victory march to see the chaos his people were bestowing on his new enemy. He had never thought of leaving his land to take what others had by force. This new concept intrigued him and opened his mind for war. His black eyes glared as he day dreamed of a bloody battlefield full of carnage and death.

The men Michael set out had reached the shores of Aodhan just in time to witness the battle. After seeing the battle they quickly got back into their ship to report back to Michael before being seen. "That's the fastest turn around I've ever experienced, didn't even get to try any ales" the old fisherman said. He fell asleep and missed the battle; when he awoke the men were rowing home. Two of the men were trembling whilst they rowed their ores in an attempt to get as far away from Aodhan as possible. It did not take them long to witness the berserker army slaughtering Adeen's men. Along with some of John's, that their countrymen were not on the winning side of this war. They could smell the blood in the air from fifty yards of the shore line. The men had done their jobs and would risk the ride over the sea again; rather than to stick around and receive any information from the men of the North Capital. Michael's messengers rowed faster now than when they were entering into the storm on their way there. This time back through, the storm would barley sway their efforts on returning to the North Harbor of Carraig. They continued straight into the storm and didn't look back. They could hear the sounds of the whales, the lightning struck hard and the thunder made their hearts jump. Yet, they kept rowing out of fear of what they had seen back at Aodhan, not what was in front of them. The waves grew and they pushed over in dyer attempts to make it home.

CHAPTER XI

THE CAPTURE

Later that night Denrel led his Berserkers on a surprise attack. They had made ladders from fallen oak branches. By the time the watch men rang the bell ten Berserkers were over the castle walls. John and his men grabbed their weapons and went to the courtyard where the next battle would take place. When John arrived fifty men lay slain on the ground and more than two hundred Berserkers had flooded the castle. Amnon and his archers went to the wall and stopped them from entering the castle. Amnon lit the ladders on fire and poured oil off the side of the castle walls. Half of his archers were firing arrows over the side at Berserkers still trying to scale the wall; the other half were firing down at the ones that had already breached the castle and entered the courtyard. The Berserker army outside of the castle wall could no longer enter and help their comrades. They were forced to retreat out of range of Amnon's violent arrows. John and his men quickly finished off the remaining Berserkers except for one. Denrel had been with the first few to climb the wall and now he had no way out. After being circled by more than twenty five men he dropped his axe. John ordered him in chains and he was brought to a solid rock room with no windows and chained to the wall. John closed the wooden door and left him in the dark.

John had been caught by surprise but he felt as if it had worked to his advantage. He now had the Berserker lord in custody. After doubling the guards and setting the bodies on fire he called his Captains and King Adeen to a meeting. "What should we do with him?" John said in question. "Let's hang him off the wall" Aaron said in an excited voice. "No, we might need him. Keep him alive until this war is over; then you can have him" Simon said in a parental tone. "I Agree with Simon" John said while looking down in deep thought. The rest of the men in the council agreed and they went back to their individual chambers. John didn't know what purpose he might serve, but something inside him told him to spare his life for the time being.

John kept his men inside the castle for the next week and every day the Berserkers attacked and attempted to climb the wall. Night and day there were different attacks. Sometimes they would make it over and other day's they never got to the top of the wall. John knew this would be never ending and he would eventually have to go and face them head on again. He planned this for the next day and when morning came he opened the gates. His army sprinted for the Berserker enemy and their weapons clashed. John's men suffered the wraith of the Berserkers. They killed more of John's men in this day then in the previous week. John had no choice but to call the retreat. Aaron had been sliced in the back by a Berserker axe and would be unable to fight for at least a week.

John kept his men in the castle and allowed them to heal. The advantage of having a castle began to feel like a prison to him. Adeen's men were wearing thin and John's men had seen enough battle and war to last a life time. Morale had never been so low for John and his men. The next morning John and his men prepared for the usual attack on the wall. After many hours and the sun beating down on them John called Amnon to his side. "Have your men seen any sign of the enemy?" John asked. "Nothing" replied Amnon. For the rest of the day and into the night there was silence. John's mind began to race. He wondered if they had given up hope and left back to the Castle of Aodhan. Perhaps they were leaving the entire Kingdom he thought. Or maybe they were up to something else. He spent the better part of an hour thinking about where the enemy was or what they were doing. Before he realized it he was waking up the next morning to Amnon calling his name.

"There is a lone Berserker at the gate and he is unarmed" Amnon informed John. "He wants to speak with King John" he added. John replied "Get your archers ready and open the gate" he walked to the gate and Simon was standing behind him ready to attack in case it was a trap. The Berserker standing at the gate had scars on his face and appeared to be much older than John. He stood tall and had no fear in his eyes. Amnon had his bow aimed directly at the Berserker; he looked directly at Amnon and didn't flinch. John slowly walked out with his sword in hand. "You're the one they call King John? I haven't seen a finer adversary in many years. My men call me leader but you can call me Argoul. Where is my son?" John quickly realized this was the true leader of the Berserkers and the one he holds captive is just the son. "Your son is alive and well. If you have your men leave this Kingdom now, I will release him" John said with authority. Argoul replied with "If you give me my son now I will allow you and your men to board your ships and go back to Carraig. Oh yes, I have learned who you are. Aodhan villagers tell all when they have an axe in their face" John looked surprised and answered his request with "That will not happen. You have my terms! take them or leave them" John stood tall and showed the Berserker King that he did not fear him or his men. "I have five hundred of my best with me and another six thousand waiting in the Black Wood of Adlarikr. If you do not release my son you will burn" Argoul snarled as he turned and walked away.

John also turned and went back into the castle. Simon met him half way and asked what had been said. After John told him, Simon looked determined. Not determined that he would win this fight but determined to win or die trying. That night the war cries of the Berserkers could be heard throughout the castle. Soon after, balls of hay and grass lit on fire sailed over the castle walls. A fire started within the castle and soldiers scrambled to put it out. While John's men tried putting out the fire; Berserkers climbed the wall. These Berserkers wielded different weapons, not everyone carried an axe. Some had swords others had spears. John ran to the wall and was met with a long spear that pierced his side. He swiftly defended himself and struck down his enemy. His wound affected him and within five minutes he collapsed to the ground. His vision began to get blurry and his hand lost the strength to carry his sword. Slowly he lost consciousness and passed out from fatigue and blood loss. Amnon spotted him lying on the ground and ordered two of his archers to carry him to safety. Marcus witnessed the two archers carrying his king and immediately ran over to assist. He pulled John to a secure location and left him with his fellow soldiers to guard him. Marcus then returned to the battle. Simon took full charge and rallied his troops to push back the invading force. This took time but was a success. Amnon had fired one last arrow at the enemy. He turned to give aide to Simon but a Berserker warrior had been spying him on the wall. He snuck up behind Amnon and grabbed him across the chest. Amnon struggled to get free but just as he was nearly loose; another Berserker grabbed him as well. All three went over the wall. The Berserkers broke Amnon's fall to a certain extent. However, a small company of Berserker soldiers saw this and went for Amnon. They carried him into the dark and took his weapons.

John woke three days later next to Aaron. Aaron gave a half hearted smile and said "Well, we've lost more than half of our men. Good news is we killed a bunch of theirs too. So in the long run if we die they die too" John usually would have laughed at this but his side was in too much pain. "Oh, one more thing, Amnon was pulled over the wall and no one knows if he is alive or dead" Aaron said in a serious voice this time. John laid back and took a deep breath "I'm going to take Argoul up on his offer. We're going home" Aaron looked down and said "It's too late for that. If we give up his son after you told him the terms; he will kill us anyway" John threw his hands up and said "Then what do we do Aaron? Do we ride out and have one last battle to our deaths?" Aaron looked back at John and with a hesitated voice replied "That's all we can do"

Simon walked in the room and said "Glad you're awake, we need you at the wall" John managed to climb to his feet and slowly make his way to the wall. When he looked over the side he saw Amnon on his knees badly bleeding with Argoul standing over him holding an axe to the back of his head. Argoul looked up at John and said "A fair trade! My son for your man" John looked at Argoul with rage. Amnon raised his head and strained to yell "Don't do it! It's all he wants" John looked over at Simon and whispered "Get the prisoner" John then yelled down "Release him and I shall return your son" Argoul glared up at John and shouted "Whenever you're ready" John motioned to open the gate and Denrel was escorted by Simon. Simon held a long rope that was attached to Denrel's neck. Simon's horse reared up behind him as he walked towards his father. Once Simon was within twenty feet of Amnon he yelled to Argoul "Release him Berserker!" Argoul lifted his axe from Amnon and told him to go.

When Amnon passed Simon he released the rope and Denrel walked to his father. The two then disappeared in the woods. Amnon was taken to a room where John met him. The two talked about what had happened to Amnon. Amnon was kept tied to a tree far from the enemy camp. He couldn't report anything useful. Aaron could finally make his way through the castle unassisted. Between the Captains and John, they were all in bad shape. John gathered his men and began to talk to them "I want to know if you will ride out one last time with me in battle. One last fight...One final stand. We might see our last days on this land but we will all know that we delayed the attack on Carraig!" John's men rallied together and realized their fate. They were ready to die in honor.

Chapter XII

The Last Stand

The next morning John opened the gates and the rest of his army staggered out into the open. Aaron managed to put on his armor as did John. Amnon couldn't shoot his bow but he could still command his archers and wield a sword. Simon would lead the attack with his riders. The Berserkers were ready as well; Argoul took charge of them and Denrel was in the front. He wanted revenge and to regain his honor in his father's eyes. When the two armies came within a hundred yards of each other they both charged at full speed. The Berserkers began knocking down John's men left and right. Aaron stayed close to John; in his mind if they were going to die then they would die together. John couldn't move well because of his wounded side but he had many men surrounding him.

For every Berserker that died five of John's men fell. Argoul didn't fight, he just stood by and watched. Denrel smashed through his enemies with extreme violence; until he reached John on the battlefield. John's men moved aside

---

at his command and Denrel swung first. John couldn't move out of the way of Denrel's massive axe; he could only put up his sword and take the hit. Aaron was watching this duel but didn't move in to help because he felt that John would want all of the glory for this mighty kill. Although, in the back of Aaron's mind, he feared John might be too weak to defeat his opponent.

Just then John took a swift blow to the arm which cut him from his shoulder down to his hand. This new wound didn't seem to bother him; he was too focused to pay attention to the pain. Argoul walked up to witness his son in combat. Many men had now fallen and the Berserkers were looking unchallenged. Adeen looked in dismay at the battle from the wall of the castle. John's wound had reopened and he was bleeding from his side. He fell to one knee and grabbed his side. Denrel saw his opportunity and lifted his axe high above his head. He glanced at his father and saw a smile on his face. When he came down with his axe John mustered his energy and lunged forward forcing his sword through Denrel's stomach and out of his back. Denrel dropped his axe behind him and looked down at his fatal wound. Argoul yelled in disbelief "Nooo!" he then yelled a command to his men "Kill them! Kill them all!" Aaron hobbled to John's side and the Berserker army closed in around them.

"This is it John, we die together my King" Aaron said with a sense of pride. John smiled at him with blood dripping from his mouth and said "Together my brother" Simon was riding hard towards them when a Berserker axe flew through the air and landed in the side of his horse's neck. Simon flew off of his horse and landed harshly on the ground; a few of his riders circled him and protected him while he rose to his feet. When all hope seemed lost… a horn blew from the shore line. It was the East trumpet of Carraig…

Michael and two thousand of his men flooded the beach of Aodhan. The horn blew continuously as the riders from the East Capital sprinted to the battle; Michael led the charge. John and Aaron looked up just in time to see Michael fly past them laying waste to the Berserkers that surrounded them. Over one thousand of Michael's foot soldiers were running to John's aide. The Berserkers held their ground as Michael's riders sliced through them. John and Aaron both rose to their feet and watched as Michael's men of the East slaughtered the Berserkers. Many of the Berserkers took at least one man with them before their lives ended but it wouldn't be enough. Michael's fresh soldiers ransacked the Berserker army's forces.

Argoul saw this and called his men back. For the first time in Berserker record they ran away from the battle. Only five hundred Berserkers remained and Argoul led them back towards the Castle of Aodhan. Michael's riders followed them for almost a mile cutting down the slower ones and assuring there were no more waiting to retaliate.

Michael rode back to John and helped him inside the castle. They sat together and John began to tell him about the events that took place in the last three months. All of John's men that remained cleaned their wounds and prepared their things to head home. John had his side and arm sewn up and Aaron stayed by his side. Amnon and Simon sat with each other and discussed their plans for home. Michael told John that he would ride to the Castle of Aodhan and finish off the Berserkers. John replied with

"Be careful they are not to be underestimated" Michael smiled and said "Don't worry brother, I have the best riders in Carraig" John smirked at the comment and thought to himself "So did I".

Adeen prepared to ride with Michael and reclaim his castle with what was left of his men. That afternoon Michael and one thousand of his riders set out for the Castle of Aodhan. Adeen and his men followed behind. After two days past Michael led the charge to the castle. When he arrived the castle was empty with the exception of ten soldiers Calder had left behind. They were hung for their crimes by Adeen. Michael was led to the South Harbor by one of Adeen's men just in time to see the last Berserker ship cross the horizon.

Michael and his men helped Adeen and his men clean up the castle and refortify the gate. They spent three days making it worthy enough to withstand a new attack. On the fourth day Michael prepared to ride back to Alexander and rejoin his brother. John was beginning to mend as were the rest of his men. They were more than ready to sail home and rejoin their families. The Castle of Alexander was to be left in the care of a man Adeen selected. John made his rounds to his men and assured them they would be home soon. Michael had found Curtis's body and paid it proper respects before lighting it on a mound of oak from the old gate.

When Michael and his riders returned they were greeted by John and Simon at the gate. Han and Edmond were made Captains and as their final gesture before riding down to Adeen; they caught two giant elk. That night before the men of Carraig sailed home they would feast in their victory. The feast was short lived; most of the men still needed rest and were passed out asleep early in the night. John found the thirteen year old boy that had carved the message for his father on his front door. John saw him and his father making their way to the gate to head home. This put a smile on his face, as did seeing Harold over in the courtyard petting Roman and Cain.

The next morning the ships were loaded and the men set sail. John sailed with Michael and his other Captains. John told Michael about the rough ride over and Michael couldn't believe the tale of the white sharks. John asked him "How did you make it over to Aodhan so easily?" Michael looked back at him and said "I had a guide. Some old fisherman" For the next one hundred and twenty hours the Sea of Arrachtaigh was calm and smooth. On the fifth day all of the ships reached the Port of the North and the men climbed out and stepped foot on the long awaited soil of Carraig. John had never been so happy; he knew that it would only be a short distance to see his queen and his children. Due to his injury's it would take the longest it ever had to travel from the harbor to his castle. John didn't mind this, he had dreamed about this moment since his first night at sea in the very beginning of this war. He could see Elaine in his mind and couldn't wait for her embrace.

The men from the North gathered their things and slowly made their long awaited march home. Michael and his men of the East escorted John and his Captains towards the North Capital. Despite their wounds John and his men were ecstatic while they walked to their families and to their homes. Aaron looked at John and smiled "You did it John. You led the men of the North to a victory" as John looked back at Aaron he said "We led them to victory. I couldn't have done it without my Captains" that was the last words they said to one another for the rest of the journey to the mighty Castle of Sumerled.

When John came within view of his castle his heart was overjoyed with the thought of seeing Elaine and his sons. The bell began to ring from the castle and Elaine ran to the castle wall. When she looked over the wall she saw John in front of two thousand men. She immediately had the gate opened and went to the bottom of the wall. Brian and Cahal were playing in the courtyard; when they heard the bells they ran to the gate. Brian was the first to see his father approaching. He ran to the stable were his horse was already saddled. Brian leaped on his horse and began to gallop towards his father. Simon was next to John and leaned over to him "Your son has grown" John smiled proudly and responded with "He has and by the looks of it; he is already a better rider than both of us"

Brian approached John with a huge smile on his face and pulled his horse along side of him. "Father! Did you win the battle?" he said in excitement. But before John could answer he saw the men behind him. Most of them were bandaged up and walking with a look of joy masking a feeling of loss and despair. Brian could see on the faces of the men that this war had taken many lives. He regretted asking his father such a question before looking around at the obvious. John looked at him and said "We had a well earned victory that cost many lives of our men"

John could see that Brian felt remorse and quickly changed the conversation "How are your mother and brother doing?" Brian felt a small amount of ease and replied "Mother has missed you; she talks about you all the time.

Cahal has been riding everyday and can nearly beat me in a race, nearly" John smiled at him as they were about to pass the gate and with a low sincere voice said "It's good to see you son" Brian smiled back and followed with "It's good to see you too father"

Elaine ran to John and embraced him. She squeezed him so tightly that he groaned in pain from the wound on his side. She quickly let go and looked down at his side "You're hurt" she said in a frantic voice. "No, I'm fine it's just a little flesh wound" he said not to discourage her. Elaine pulled him in close again not so tightly and the two interlocked lips. They stood there together for all to see; John had missed her and she had missed him. For the first time in months everything was as it should be for the King and Queen of North Carraig. Elaine interlocked her arm with his and they walked together. John gave orders to his men to help the wounded and he sent out messengers to inform the Kingdom of their return and victory. John went straight for his father's chair in the great hall. He had his bear skin mounted above the mantle. He sat there with Elaine the entire night and told her stories of the war. He left out many parts as not to worry her; he also left out the parts that bothered him. He never spoke to her or anyone of Curtis. His heart was in great pain from the loss of his friend.

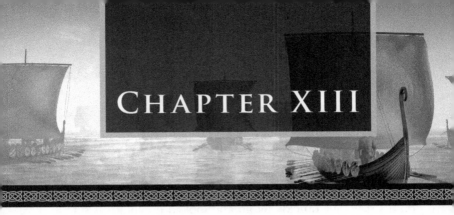

CHAPTER XIII

BACK IN CARRAIG

I t took two weeks for the men to finally feel back to normal and not on edge. Their families understood and gave the men space when they desired it. John was almost healed along with Aaron and Simon. James and a great party of men and women from the West arrived that morning. To congratulate the men on their victory over Calder and the Berserkers. John sat with James and told him of the various battles and trails he went through. After a few hours of them talking; James suggested that John declare this day as a holiday of victory. John thought about it and declined the idea. John wanted this to be a day of memory not celebration; he wanted the entire Kingdom to know what the men had died for. He explained to James that the men didn't give their lives just to keep Carraig safe but they died trying to keep the men and women of Aodhan safe as well.

Michael still had not returned to the East; in his mind he felt he needed to stay with John and offer any service he could. After a few days the trumpet from the South blew and Daniel along with his family and many men and women arrived. The four brothers sat in the great hall and discussed the plans for setting up patrols. John didn't want his men to have to do any of the patrols for the first six months while they healed and spent time with their families. Michael quickly offered to have his men continue the patrols of the North. James offered to send a large number to the East to make up for Michael's men being in the North. Daniel had such a large area to cover he could not spare any men and the four brothers agreed.

Michael then spoke out in the meeting and proposed a new law so that this loss of life in any particular Capital would never happen again. "We need a new law that states in a time of war; a High King be selected and in charge of operations" Michael said this without a hint of debate in his voice. He continued with "Never will one of our Capital's be at war while the others are not. We are not only brothers but we rule an entire Kingdom. If part of our Kingdom is at war then the entire Kingdom is at war" without hesitation James and Daniel Agreed. Michael then looked at John and said "John will be this High King in a time of war" the other brothers nodded their heads in agreement.

The brothers wrote the new war decree and then enjoyed each other's company and the company of their families. They stayed together for almost a week before Daniel packed up and headed for the South Capital. Shortly after James set out for the West and Michael too had his men pack their things and start heading for home. John hardly left Elaine's sight and when he felt up to it he would show Brian a few helpful tricks with a sword. Cahal would often be in the same vicinity watching and learning what he could. Full sized swords were still too heavy for him so he preferred a bow.

By the time fall came around John was back to his strong usual self. Simon's head made a full recovery with the exception of a thin line were his hair would not grow back. Aaron had thick battle scars but they didn't cause him pain. Amnon moved to a small house he built with a woman from the north he planned to marry. He was still in ear shot of the bells in case he was needed to assume his post as Captain of the archers. His wounds too had healed and he would shoot his bow daily for practice.

Roman and Cain were back in their usual routines of annoying Elaine. John knew his dog's worth from the war and Elaine rarely questioned him about the battles he had been in. She would let him tell her what he wanted too; which he had the first night of his return. She could see he was bothered by the amount of men he had lost. In turn she would often try to take his mind off of the thought of war. John finally understood what his father was so famous for and why he always valued his men's loyalty. John hung his armor and sword up in his room next to his bed. He would look at it and think of his fallen friends such as Curtis. He had a statue built of Curtis and placed in the courtyard. At the bottom an inscription read "Captain Curtis of the North: Fell during the war in Aodhan" many flowers had been placed at the base of this statue.

Aaron felt the most loss when it came to Curtis. Aaron knew Curtis had given his life to save him. Aaron spent more time than usual with John; he would sit in the great hall with him and talk about Curtis. From time to time

Simon would join them; none of them had any regret's from the war only a sense of sadness.

One morning John woke up and went to Brian and Cahal's room. He woke the two boys up and told them they were going for a ride. They each climbed on their horses and headed out of the castle towards the south. Behind them about one hundred yards, rode fifty armed guards. The boys listened to their father point out land marks and tell the history behind them. He took them down alongside of the river and when they reached the barge he paid the men there for a ride down. He didn't need to pay them but he felt the need to. When it came close to dark the King and his sons got off the barge and made camp.

The next morning they got up with the sun and rode until noon. John continued to point out things his father had shown him and describe their significance. Soon they came in front of a road that led to a large castle. This was the Castle of Sechnaill; Michael heard the bells from his castle ringing and looked out from the top of his castle wall to see his brother and two nephews riding down the road. It had been a long time since John had made the trip down to the East Capital. Michael yelled with his booming voice "Lower the gate!" immediately the gate lowered to the ground.

John, Brian, and Cahal rode in the castle. Not far behind were John's guards; they quickened their pace once John cleared the castle's gate. Michael came to greet them as did his daughter Cara. Michael told his servants to prepare a feast for his brother's arrival. When Michael sat down with John after they had put the horses in the stable he asked "What do I owe the honor?" John turned and smiled at Michael "I haven't been down here in a very long time. I just wanted to see what you had done to this place" Michael laughed when he heard this and replied "It hasn't changed much" John looked around and agreed "No, it really hasn't"

The two feasted together long into the night. Brian and Cahal each were given their own extravagant rooms. Before long the entire castle was silent and everyone slept. The next morning during their first meal a soldier came to Michael. He reported that there were a few fishermen at the gate; they had pulled into the East Harbor the night before. They were requesting an audience with Michael. Michael didn't care to be bothered during a meal so he told them to wait in the courtyard. A few hours later Michael realized he had forgotten all about them and rushed to the courtyard to give his apologies.

The men were still waiting and gladly accepted the apology. The oldest one began by saying "King Michael we are fishermen from Adalrikr. We usually travel from there to Aodhan and then over to Carraig. When we were getting ready to venture to Aodhan we were stopped by King Arvid's men" one of the other men interrupted "They asked us where we were going and why. After we told them, they said there had been a war that had taken place" then the older fisherman took the conversation back "As we prepared to set sail, we overheard the soldiers talking to one another about a six thousand man Berserker army preparing to move out from the Black Wood. We thought while we did our trading in Carraig that perhaps we could get paid for the information"

Michael looked at John as he reached in his pocket; he paid the two men ten silver coins. They thanked Michael and all of the fishermen went on their way. Michael asked

John "Do you think they are coming for us?" John's face showed concern as he replied "Where ever they are going won't be good. If they go to Aodhan, it will fall quickly. If they come here many of our people will die a brutal death"

John and Michael sat together and discussed their options. John had no intention of leaving Carraig again this soon. Michael brought up the concern that if the Berserkers attacked an entire Kingdom with that much force; other Kingdoms would prepare for war as well. He believed that such a war could turn every Kingdom against one another. John agreed and sent out messengers to James and Daniel. He called his guards and had all fifty of them escort Brian and Cahal back to Elaine in the North Capital.

THE HIGH KING'S
DECISION

Within ten days James and Daniel made it to the East Capital. When they saw John and Michael standing over a table that had maps of all the Kingdoms; they knew something had happened. John and Michael informed the other king's about the news they had heard. James tried to calm everyone down by telling them that this could have been a scheme for money by the fishermen. John didn't deny this but he had to be sure. John ordered a scout ship to sneak into Adalrikr and inform them of the Berserker activity. Michael brought up the idea to send ships to the other Kingdoms and inform them of the situation.

They agreed and James sent out a ship to the Kingdom of Adair which was west of Carraig. Daniel sent out two ships; one to the Kingdom of Hag and the other to what was left of Dolg. Michael sent out a ship to Aodhan. This messenger was tasked with asking Adeen if he would be willing to get his people and come to Carraig for safety. John knew that if the Berserkers landed in Aodhan again; the entire Kingdom would surely fall.

After warning the entire Kingdom of what may be coming; John, Daniel, and James headed home. The only thing any of them could do now was to wait for their scout's to return with news. John traveled alone to the North Capital. This had been the first time he had ever traveled through Carraig by himself. He enjoyed the trip unaccompanied. John let his mind wonder and day dreamed about old times he had with his father.

All of Carraig were standing by on high alert. The soldiers that guarded the borders of Carraig had been doubled. Any able bodied men that were not soldiers were told to be ready to go to their nearest castle and give aide in case of an invasion. All households began to store food and water in case they were forced to stay in their homes.

When John made it home Elaine asked him for news. He was very reluctant to tell her but he did anyway. She seemed to be casual about the new information for John's sake. Elaine could see that John looked overwhelmed. She would bring him hot tea as he sat in the great hall studying maps and preparing battle strategies. This lasted for nearly two weeks before the messenger that had been sent to Aodhan returned.

Upon his arrival he sat before John and his Captains and explained what Adeen had told him "The King of Aodhan refused to leave his homeland. However, he sent messengers to both the Kingdoms of Dolg and Hag, asking them to send soldiers. He also would like soldiers from Carraig as well" John looked angered at the news and replied with

"Adeen is stubborn and will pay for his stupidity. I will not send anymore men to die in Aodhan. If he will not come here to safety then he will be over run and destroyed"

John then told the messenger to inform his brothers of the news. Within three hours the messenger rode out to the other Capitals. All seemed normal in Carraig with the exception of the traveling soldiers as they changed over their patrol watch. After a few more weeks went by the messengers from Dolg and Hag returned. The High King of Hag told the messenger that he would not be sparing any of his soldiers to Adeen for the fact that he had already lent half of them to help rebuild Dolg after Calder had destroyed most of it. He appreciated the news from John and awarded the messenger with gold and silver. Most of the soldiers in Dolg had been wiped out and they too would not be sending soldiers to the aide of Adeen.

John knew that this would be the end of Adeen and perhaps all of Aodhan if the rumors of the Berserker army had been true. John considered sending a messenger to Adalrikr to offer terms of peace between the two but after consulting with Aaron and Simon he decided this would be folly. John could only wait for his scouts to return from Adalrikr and see if the rumors were true. Three more weeks passed and one morning John was awakened by bells and trumpets. He went to the castle wall and saw Daniel riding in alongside of James and Michael. John ran to the gate to see what news they brought. The brothers had cold looks on their faces and went straight for the great hall. John greeted them and asked "What news?" Daniel began by saying "Our scouts that were sent to Adalrikr were found this morning" John looked confused and said "Found? What do you mean?" with a cold look of malice Daniel answered "My soldiers from the South Harbor spotted a ship from southeast that was on fire. When my ships reached the wreckage the only thing found floating in the water were the bodies of my scouts tied to the mast"

John looked at his three brothers and said "They are coming then" Daniel looked back at John and replied "I showed Michael the axe that was stuck into the mast and he confirmed it was from the Berserkers". James sat quietly for a moment and then spoke out to the group "This was an act of war. John, you are the High King. Do we wait for them to come or do we travel to Adalrikr and strike?" All eyes were on John now; it was now up to him to decide.

As John was about to give his decision Simon and Aaron walked into the great hall. Behind them came Elaine, Brian, and Cahal. They all could tell from the look on the faces of their King's; that an eminent danger was now upon them. John allowed them to sit at the table and listen to the alternatives that he and his brothers conversed over. They spent more than three hours weighing their options. Daniel suggested an all out assault on Adalrikr. His judgment may have been clouded by the anger he felt from the inhumane death of his scouts. James had no opinion; he was ready to do whatever John decided. His remorse in not helping his brother in the beginning still haunted him. Michael and John seemed to be in congruence with each other. They both felt that they should wait for the Berserkers to attack because they were unfamiliar with the landscape of Carraig. This is exactly what John did not want to happen but he had little choice.

After discussing their options John concluded the conversation with "I know what we face and I know what will happen if we let them come. However, if we leave Carraig to rage war we will need every man we have. In turn, Carraig will be left defenseless and if we should fail to defeat our enemy then all the lives left in Carraig will be slain. Our allies are on the brink of extinction and cannot help us. We are on our own but we are strong and will survive any attack that may be upon us"

The End

CPSIA information can be obtained
at www.ICGtesting.com
Printed in the USA
BVHW071554100919
558045BV00003B/415/P